"I [...]
wa[...]
a man likes to hear flattering remarks
from a lovely woman."

"Really?" she said, breathless.

"Yes. Most men won't admit it but we love having our egos stroked."

"I mean, do you really think I'm lovely?"

"Yes." That smile again. She reveled in it, bathed in it, got lost in it. Then, ever so slowly Lance leaned toward her, and she got so nervous and excited she nearly fell off her chair.

He was going to kiss her. She could see it coming, feel it, taste it. She was actually getting ready to pucker up when he rubbed the side of her mouth with his thumb.

"You have chocolate." Oh, Lord, his hand on her face felt wonderful, miraculous. She wished she had chocolate from head to toe.

Dear Reader,

As you ski into the holiday season, be sure to pick up the latest batch of Silhouette Special Edition romances. Featured this month is Annette Broadrick's latest miniseries, SECRET SISTERS, about family found after years of separation. The first book in this series is *Man in the Mist* (#1576), which Annette describes as "…definitely a challenge to write." About her main characters, Annette says, "Greg, the wounded lion hero—you know the type—gave me and the heroine a very hard time. But we refused to be intimidated and, well, you'll see what happened!"

You'll adore this month's READERS' RING pick, *A Little Bit Pregnant* (SE#1573), which is an emotional best-friends-turned-lovers tale by reader favorite Susan Mallery. *Her Montana Millionaire* (SE#1574) by Crystal Green is part of the popular series MONTANA MAVERICKS: THE KINGSLEYS. Here, a beautiful socialite dazzles the socks off a dashing single dad, but gets her own lesson in love. Nikki Benjamin brings us the exciting conclusion of the baby-focused miniseries MANHATTAN MULTIPLES, with *Prince of the City* (SE#1575). Two willful individuals, who were lovers in the past, have become bitter enemies. Will they find their way back to each other?

Peggy Webb tantalizes our romantic taste buds with *The Christmas Feast* (SE#1577), in which a young woman returns home for Christmas, but doesn't bargain on meeting a man who steals her heart. And don't miss *A Mother's Reflection* (SE#1578), Elissa Ambrose's powerful tale of finding long-lost family…and true love.

These six stories will enrich your hearts and add some spice to your holiday season. Next month, stay tuned for more page-turning and provocative romances from Silhouette Special Edition.

Happy reading!

Gail Chasan
Senior Editor

Please address questions and book requests to:
Silhouette Reader Service
U.S.: 3010 Walden Ave., P.O. Box 1325, Buffalo, NY 14269
Canadian: P.O. Box 609, Fort Erie, Ont. L2A 5X3

The Christmas Feast

PEGGY WEBB

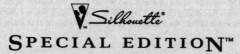

SPECIAL EDITION™

Published by Silhouette Books

America's Publisher of Contemporary Romance

To Joli Elizabeth Estes on her graduation.

and

To Michael, forever.

 SILHOUETTE BOOKS

ISBN 0-373-24577-7

THE CHRISTMAS FEAST

Copyright © 2003 by Peggy Webb.

This edition published by arrangement with Harlequin Books S.A.

® and TM are trademarks of Harlequin Books S.A., used under license.
Trademarks indicated with ® are registered in the United States Patent
and Trademark Office, the Canadian Trade Marks Office and in other
countries.

Visit Silhouette at www.eHarlequin.com

Printed in U.S.A.

Books by Peggy Webb

Silhouette Special Edition

Summer Hawk #1300
Warrior's Embrace #1323
Gray Wolf's Woman #1347
Standing Bear's Surrender #1384
Invitation to a Wedding #1402
*The Smile of an Angel #1436
*Bittersweet Passion #1449
*Force of Nature #1461
†The Accidental Princess #1516
†The Mona Lucy #1534
The Christmas Feast #1577

Silhouette Romance

When Joanna Smiles #645
A Gift for Tenderness #681
Harvey's Missing #712
Venus DeMolly #735
Tiger Lady #785
Beloved Stranger #824
Angel at Large #867

*The Westmoreland Diaries
†The Foxes

Silhouette Intimate Moments

13 Royal Street #447

Silhouette Books

Silhouette Christmas Stories
"I Heard the Rabbits Singing"

PEGGY WEBB

and her two chocolate Labs live in a hundred-year-old house not far from the farm where she grew up. "A farm is a wonderful place for dreaming," she says. "I used to sit in the hayloft and dream of being a writer." Now, with two grown children and more than forty-five romance novels to her credit, the former English teacher confesses she's still a hopeless romantic and loves to create the happy endings her readers love so well.

When she isn't writing, she can be found at her piano playing blues and jazz or in one of her gardens planting flowers. A believer in the idea that a person should never stand still, Peggy recently taught herself carpentry.

Jolie's Favorite Chocolate Pie

1 stick butter
1 cup sugar
5 tbsp self-rising flour
3 small or medium-size eggs, well beaten
1 6-oz bag of semisweet chocolate chips
whipped cream

Preheat oven to 350°F. Melt butter in a medium-size baking dish in the microwave. Remove dish, then add sugar, flour and eggs to melted butter. Mix well. Add chocolate chips. Bake for approximately 40 minutes. Remove, let cool and serve with dollops of whipped cream.

Chapter One

"If I can read, I can cook."

Jolie Katherine Coltrane said this aloud three times. She needed all the boosting she could get. She was in the formerly pristine O'Banyon mansion kitchen, standing ankle-deep in soapy water.

She'd let the suds run over the rim of the sink, where she'd piled twenty-odd pots and pans that would probably never be clean again. "Except by a joint act of Congress and God," she said, then glared at the dirty dishes as if she could browbeat them into submission.

Meanwhile the turtle soup that was supposed to be creamy and delicious was turning purple in the pot.

The garlic roasted potatoes looked like kidney stones, the turkey refused to open its legs to be stuffed, and eating the cake required a spoon.

"I will not be defeated!" Jolie rolled up her sleeves and set to work with the mop. As soon as she found the floor she was going to try her hand at chocolate fudge delight. Everybody loved chocolate fudge. It stood to reason that everybody could cook it.

She was still mopping when the phone rang. Slogging through the water, she banged her leg on the butcher's block table, then lost her footing and slid the rest of the way to the phone.

"Hello."

"Kat? Is that you?"

She made a face at the phone. How like Elizabeth to call in the middle of a disaster. Her older and only sister never had disasters of her own, but if she did she'd handle them without breaking a perfectly polished fingernail, let alone a sweat.

"Yes, it's me, and don't call me Kat. It makes me sound like I eat tuna out of a can on the kitchen floor. Call me Jolie."

"Why? You've never objected before."

"I'm turning over a new leaf."

"What kind of new leaf?"

Jolie wasn't about to reveal her plans. She would triumph or fail on her own, thank you very much. Not that Elizabeth would do or say anything to make her feel bad. On the contrary, her sister was loving and kind. The only trouble was she and everybody else in the family had cast Jolie in the role of cute, funny kid sister, the one who would always stand in the shadow of her smart, successful siblings.

Jolie was tired of shadows and sick to death of being cute and funny. But instead of saying that, she told Elizabeth, "I don't know. I haven't figured out which leaf to turn over yet…"

Jolie sighed. Here she was, stymied by the simple task of cooking while Elizabeth was filming documentaries that changed lives and saved third world countries.

"It's your age, isn't it?"

"What does my age have to do with anything?"

"Twenty-nine is dangerous."

"I didn't see you dodging bullets and evading flying missiles when you were my age."

"Yes, but you and I are different."

"You can say that again."

"Gosh, Kat, you *are* down, aren't you?"

"No, not really. You forgot to call me Jolie."

"Okay, *Jolie*. Tell your big sister what's bothering you."

"We're on long distance."

"That's okay. I can afford it."

"That's just it. You and Matt are rich and successful, and look at me. I turned out all wrong."

"No, you didn't. You're a cute, funny, compassionate young woman who has turned her love of animals into a profession.''

"Pet grooming is hardly a profession.''

"Well, a job then.'' During the long pause that followed, Jolie pictured Elizabeth tallying up her baby sister's pros and cons. The cons would win by a landslide. "I'll admit you've made a few mistakes along the way.''

"See? Even my own sister thinks I'm a failure.'' Jolie tucked a stray hair into the long braid that swung down her back.

Elizabeth and Matt had made contributions to society, and what had she done? Painted poodle toenails pink until she had amassed enough money to race off and see countries nobody'd ever heard of. Well, she was about to change all that...starting as soon as she heard whether or not she'd landed the job she'd applied for—publicity staff person with the Society for the Prevention of Cruelty to Animals. She wouldn't be saving third world countries, but at least she'd be saving some of the world's animals.

Jolie glared at the dirty dishes as if she expected them to rise up and taunt her.

"What are you doing, Jolie?''

"Practicing.''

"Practicing what?''

"Christmas dinner. I'm cooking this year.... Elizabeth, are you still there?''

"I'm coming out of shock. Is Aunt Kitty still at Cousin Josh's?"

"Yes. It'll take them a while to move his stuff into a new parsonage. I don't need Aunt Kitty or anybody to help me. I'm going to do this all by myself."

"If it doesn't work out we can always pick up something at the deli."

"See? That's just what I mean. Nobody ever expects anything of me except giving Bijons a new hairdo. Not only am I going to cook a fabulous feast, I'm going to learn Swahili."

"Why would you want to learn a language that won't do you a bit of good? Why don't you learn Spanish? We border Mexico, and Florida and the Southwest are filled with Spanish-speaking people."

Jolie decided then and there she'd learn French. Not because she fancied it over Spanish, but because Elizabeth hadn't suggested it. It irked her that her older sister was always right. Jolie planned to change that, too. Before she was finished with the reinvention of Jolie Katherine Coltrane, perfect strangers would be stopping her on the street for advice.

About what, she didn't know. She'd figure it out later. After she whipped the kitchen back into shape and got a good fudge recipe under her belt.

"I'm going to do this my way, Elizabeth," she said evasively, before asking, "When will you be coming home?"

"It's going to take at least another week to wrap up this film, but a friend of mine will arrive soon, probably tomorrow. I thought he might already be there. I was calling to make sure he's comfortable."

"A boyfriend?"

"A nice guy. Make him welcome. Take care, kid."

"But Elizabeth—"

"I've got to run, Kat. They need me on the set."

The phone went dead. Elizabeth had hung up without giving a single particular about her friend. Well, why not? Nobody in her family ever treated Jolie as if she had a lick of sense. They patted her head and talked over her or around her, but never to her. Not really. They all acted as if she were still a toddler with drool on her chin.

She'd show them. After she'd mastered cooking and foreign languages, and got her new Job With Potential, she was going back to night school to earn a degree in… Oh, she didn't know what. Something important. Medicine or forestry or engineering. That was it. She'd design rockets and her name would be engraved on a brass plaque and placed in a space center somewhere. Maybe even in Washington, D.C.

"First the fudge."

She turned on the radio. Maybe that was the reason for her earlier failure. She'd needed music. Everything was better with some good rock 'n' roll.

Sure enough, she made quick work of the floor,

then decided to leave the dirty pots soaking till tomorrow.

Using the last clean pot in the kitchen, she set about making fudge. She sang along with Elvis and rock'abillied with Jerry Lee Lewis, and before she knew it she had a batch of hot chocolate that looked as if it just might congeal into candy.

She moved the skillet off the range and headed toward the library to get a book to read while the fudge cooled. She plucked one of her mother's romance novels off the shelves, *Silk and Shadows,* a favorite of Jolie's and one she'd already read twice. The novel was a vivid reminder that everybody in Jolie's family had succeeded except her. Her mother was a famous novelist, her sister was an award-winning filmmaker and her brother a renowned lawyer.

As she headed back to the kitchen, she froze. What was that sound?

It came again, and she saw the shadowy branches of the overgrown camellia rubbing against the windowpane.

Relieved, Jolie danced her way to the kitchen until what she saw through the window panel in the kitchen door stopped her in her tracks. Silhouetted there was a man with long hair. Good grief, an intruder! And she couldn't even dial 9ll. No way could she stand there in plain view and chat with the police. Where was her cell phone when she needed it?

She ducked behind the cooking island, then crept into the utility room to look for a weapon.

Lance hadn't meant to break and enter.

Elizabeth had given him a key and assured him the house would be empty. "Mom and Ben are in L.A. visiting Aunt Dolly," she'd said. Dolly Wilder, the movie star. Not really Elizabeth's aunt, but a sorority sister of her mother's and such a frequent guest to O'Banyon Manor that the children called her "aunt."

"Aunt Kitty is visiting her son." That was Kitty O'Banyon, the eccentric widowed aunt who lived with Elizabeth's mom. "Matt and his wife are in Jackson on a case he can't leave." The brother, apparently like his sister, driven and successful. "And God knows where Kat is. Probably off chasing another wild hare." The ditzy sister. Not Elizabeth's words, but his own, judging by everything she had told him.

All in all, borrowing somebody else's family for the holidays promised to make it an interesting Christmas.

That's what he'd been thinking when he parked his motorcycle under the magnolia tree and mounted the front steps of the most impressive home in Shady Grove, the *only* impressive place in this small, backwater Mississippi town.

A penlight flashed briefly in the darkness inside

the house, and footsteps only a man trained for stealth could have heard whispered along the floor.

This was a high season for burglary, and the well-kept O'Banyon Manor would be a prime target. Lance listened long enough to track the burglar's movements, then pocketed the key Elizabeth had given him. He would go in the back way and take him by surprise. His gun was still in his knapsack, but he didn't plan on using it. His size and his martial arts training would be the only weapons he needed.

It took him a while to make his way around the enormous multiwinged mansion and through a series of gardens and courtyards, but then he saw another light, blazing through kitchen windows.

"Good." He was dealing with a careless burglar. Or one who hated the dark.

He heard the music before he saw the slight figure doing what appeared to be a Native American war dance, long braid flying. It was either the smallest, stupidest accomplice Lance had ever seen or else the youngest.

He would dispatch the kid with ease. The mansion was so big that unless the accomplice set up a huge ruckus, the burglar in the east wing of the house would never hear.

Lance picked the lock swiftly on the kitchen door, then stepped into a war zone. Without the warrior. Where had that kid gone?

Before he could get his bearings he was set upon by a smudged waif wielding a mop.

She whacked his knees so hard the blow brought tears. Before he could grab her, she started beating him around the head with such fury he thought he was caught up in a blender.

What kind of thief carried a mop? Not the dangerous kind, obviously. He could have pinned her to the floor in no time flat, but he didn't make a practice of harming women and children, so he grabbed for the mop-wielding arm.

She ducked out of reach and came toward him with a cast-iron skillet. "Take that, you big bully."

He hardly felt the blow, but he took umbrage at the large globs of gooey chocolate she left behind.

"Hey, now...cut that out. This is my best leather jacket."

"Aha!" Without further ado she sent the skillet sailing toward his head. He ducked and made a grab for the fighting virago.

He might have put an end to this little contest in no time if he hadn't stepped into a puddle of soapy water. His feet flew out from under him and he crash-landed against the refrigerator. Before he could regain his balance, the iron skillet connected with his skull.

"Gotcha, you thief!"

Chapter Two

Jolie would have gloated except for one teensy, disturbing detail: she'd killed him. She was leaning over the burglar to check for his pulse when he came back from the dead.

Before she could move he had her in a body lock with his hand over her mouth. She kicked and twisted and jerked, but she might as well have been a fly caught on sticky paper. He was at least twice her size, with arms like oak trees and hands the size of Virginia hams.

"Be still," he said. "I'm not going to hurt you unless you scream. Is that clear?"

"*Mmmft,*" she replied, but that must not have satisfied him because he tightened his hold.

"My hands are lethal weapons. Do you understand?"

"*Urrrnd.*" She nodded so there would be no mistaking her answer.

"Good. Now I'm going to take my hand off your mouth and you're going to tell me what you're doing here."

He eased his hand away, but it took her a while to get her breath.

"Well?"

"This is my family's home," she said.

"Try again."

Lordy, he didn't believe her. Now *he* was going to kill *her*. Well, she might as well die fighting. She bit his arm, hard, and when he loosened his grip she scrambled across the kitchen and grabbed the first thing she could find—a potful of soapy water.

Taking aim, she hit her target squarely in the face. "Ha!" she yelled. She hadn't played pitcher in girls' high school baseball for nothing.

Unfortunately, the soapy water did nothing more than madden him. He lunged and both of them went down in an untidy heap. Jolie tried to scramble away, but she was no match for the raging bull who had invaded her kitchen.

Again pinned underneath him with his hand over her mouth, she figured she was going to have the life choked out of her.

"I'm going to say this one more time—I don't want to hurt you, but I will if I have to."

Think, Jolie told herself. What were her chances of survival if she simply complied?

"Understood?" he added, and she nodded as vigorously as she could, considering that she was underneath a mountain with one whole summit clamped over her mouth.

"Now, who are you and what are you doing here?"

When he released her mouth, she gulped air and talked as fast as she could. "Jolie Kat Coltrane. I live here."

"Oh, my God." She'd never seen a big man move with such alacrity. "I am so sorry." He picked her up as easily as if she were an express package left mistakenly on the floor. "Did I hurt you?"

She thought about socking him in the eye, but the look on his face stopped her. Obviously, his concern was sincere. Also, quite obviously, he knew she belonged at O'Banyon Manor, which meant he was not a burglar at all but...

"Tell me you're not Elizabeth's friend," she said.

"I'm Elizabeth's friend. Lance Estes."

"Oh, Lord, she's going to kill me."

"No, she won't. She'll never know." He set her down and started toward the hall.

"Wait, where are you going?"

"To catch a thief, if he's still there. Stay put."

"No way." Jolie grabbed the mop and trailed along behind.

Lance would have laughed if he didn't have a burglar to catch. "Can you be quiet?"

"As a headache." She grinned at him.

Maybe Elizabeth was wrong, he thought. Jolie Kat Coltrane had guts and wit, two qualities rarely present in featherheads.

"Okay," he said. "Stay behind me and don't do anything with that mop unless I say so. Got that?"

"Aye, aye, sir." She gave him a smart salute.

Elizabeth had been right about one thing: her sister was cute. Wide blue eyes and generous mouth. Stubborn chin offset by classic cheekbones. He catalogued those details as naturally as he breathed. As an agent of the elite International Security Force, he was trained to study people inside and out. And what he saw of Elizabeth's baby sister said substance, not fluff.

That pleased Lance. Since he was going to be trapped with a companion instead of having the mansion to himself until the rest of the O'Banyons and Coltranes arrived, he was glad to have somebody with enough sense to carry on a decent conversation. Maybe he'd get lucky and she would also enjoy chess or bridge.

With instincts honed to a fine point, he made his way through O'Banyon Manor and into a cavernous room whose centerpiece was a thirteen-foot-tall

Christmas tree. Broken glass crunched underneath his feet and light spilled through the wide-open front door.

"He's gone," he said.

"How do you know? He could still be lurking around here somewhere, waiting to slit our throats."

"He left the front door open. We must have scared him off with our ruckus in the kitchen."

There was no need for her or any of the family to know about his job. Elizabeth had said she wouldn't tell. "After all you've been through, you deserve an ordinary Christmas," she'd said.

Suddenly Jolie bolted past him and knelt beneath the tree. "He stole the presents."

An image of his childhood Christmases came to Lance—the tree decorated with strings of popcorn, the crate of apples donated by the local grocer underneath, the housemom complaining about the view of the parched Arizona desert outside their window. The founders of the orphanage had optimistically named it Sunshine Acres.

Empathy wrenched him until his professionalism reasserted itself. The burglar wasn't necessarily a destitute father desperate to give his family a good Christmas. He could be someone out to spoil the holidays for the town's most prominent citizens. Or a thief with a warped sense of humor. Or kids on a lark.

"He even stole some of the decorations." Jolie

picked up the pieces of a broken glass bauble. "I guess we should call the police."

That's all he needed. Law enforcement everywhere. Cameras, reporters, more headlines in the newspaper.

"There's no need. I can take care of this."

"You can?"

"Yes, but not tonight." He didn't want to trample evidence in the dark. "Let's go to bed and start fresh in the morning."

Jolie thought about his proposal for a while, then said, "Okay." He liked that—a woman who had sense enough to recognize authority without asking a lot of silly questions.

"I guess you'll want a bath, too."

"I guess." He grinned at her.

"Sorry about the chocolate."

"It's okay. At least I'll never forget this trip."

"And thanks."

"For what?"

"For not telling Elizabeth. She thinks…" Suddenly Jolie drew herself up like a soldier, hanging on to the mop as if it were a rifle. Any minute he expected her to salute. "I'll put you in the west wing," she said.

"Where do you sleep?"

"East wing."

"I'll sleep there, then." Her cheeks colored as if he'd suggested hanky-panky. He hastened to set her straight. "In the hall, if necessary. You've had one intruder tonight. I want to be close by in case you have another."

"Oh…" She flushed again. Good lord, the woman had thought he meant to sleep in her bed. "Well, of course…that's a good idea. But there's no need for you to sleep in the hall. O'Banyon Manor has too many beds for that. Follow me."

It wasn't hard to do her bidding. She had the loose, swinging walk of a tomboy, with more than a hint of sass. Lance liked Jolie's walk. In fact, there were a lot of things he liked about her.

He chose the bedroom next to hers.

"If you hear anything, just knock on the connecting door," he told her.

"Sure thing. Good night, Lance." The way she looked up at him, flushed and expectant, put him in mind of a sixteen-year-old on her first date. The thought rattled him, and he practically bit her head off with a curt, "Good night."

He was tired, that was it. Too tired to have more than one brain cell functioning. The bed, covered with a plump green comforter, was large and inviting. He'd have climbed right in if it hadn't been for the chocolate. Sighing, he stripped off his clothes and headed toward the shower for a major cleaning job for both himself and his jacket. But Jolie's voice coming from the balcony caused emotion to slam him in the gut.

"Star light, star bright..."

Jolie Kat Coltrane was standing on the balcony wishing on a star. "Good God!" Nobody in his or her right mind believed in wishes anymore. Lance jerked his pants back on and closed the curtain.

Elizabeth would never wish on a star, but that's not why Jolie was doing it. Stars fascinated her and always had, not just their beauty but the strange, mesmerizing power of them. The pull of the heavens was so strong that she stayed on the balcony until the chill crept through her sweater.

Then she went inside to her formerly safe room, which now had a ticking bomb not two feet away.

What had made Elizabeth pick the kind of man Jolie could never resist? A wild, rugged maverick, a little on the scruffy side, a lot on the dangerous side. My Lord, she wouldn't sleep a wink thinking how easily he'd picked her up off the floor. Like a bauble he'd found in a box of Cracker Jacks.

Elizabeth usually went for the buttoned-down type, the kind of man who wouldn't be caught dead in other people's houses without his coat and tie. *Leather.* This time her sister had fallen for a man in leather.

Oh Lord, his jacket. Jolie had forgotten to tell Lance that Shady Grove had a very good dry cleaner that also specialized in leather, and she would take his jacket tomorrow to have it cleaned. She didn't want him thinking she was some kind of scatterbrain who made messes she didn't clean up.

She threw back her covers and had her hand raised to pound on Lance's door when she noted a ribbon of pink through her window. Good grief, it was already tomorrow. If she didn't quit mooning over Elizabeth's boyfriend, she was never going to get any sleep.

Maybe daylight would restore her common sense. Climbing back into bed, she pulled the covers up to her chin and said, "After all, tomorrow *is* another day." She fell asleep in the midst of her best Scarlett imitation.

O'Banyon Manor was even more impressive in the daylight than it had been at night. Sitting atop the highest hill within five miles, it commanded a panoramic view of Shady Grove, a charming little town that looked whitewashed in the sun. With three church steeples, a tree-shaded square and green storefront awnings Lance hadn't noticed as he'd whizzed down Main Street in the dark, Shady Grove could have been the set for a modern-day version of Mayberry. The *Andy Griffith Show* had been Lance's favorite TV program, though the only person who'd ever known that was dead now.

Don't think about Danny.

Instead he turned his thoughts to the odd set of tracks on the manor's sweeping drive that approached O'Banyon Manor. Small rubber tires had left tracings of charcoal and soot on the concrete, another puzzlement. This was an agrarian section of Mississippi. He'd seen nothing but soybean and cotton fields lying fallow for miles between the small towns. As far as he knew Shady Grove had not one single smokestack. The biggest employer was probably the hospital on the west side of town.

He heard Jolie before he saw her. Humming "Rudolph the Red-Nosed Reindeer" and wearing soccer pads and a baseball helmet, she came toward him with a jaunty walk that lifted his spirits. Lord knows why.

"What are you doing in that getup?"

"Flak gear." Her smile was beautiful, wide and sincere, the kind of smile that lit her whole face. She squatted beside him and her perfume wafted over him.

Flak gear and perfume. Lance suppressed a smile, then wondered if she'd worn it for him. An alarming thought.

"Flak gear?"

"In case we run into danger. This was all I had. I played all kinds of sports in high school. I guess you'd call me a tomboy."

He wouldn't. Definitely not. But he didn't tell her that. Instead he stood up. Away from her. After all, he'd been kneeling a long time and needed to stretch his legs.

Or so he told himself.

"Looks like you've found evidence," she said.

"Yes. Traces of charcoal."

"Little red wagon."

"What?"

"These tracks." When she stood up her perfume wafted over him again, and all he could think about was how she would look in a black evening gown that bared her shoulders.

"They're made by a little red wagon, a Radio Flyer. I had one just like it when I was a kid. One of my favorite things to do was run it through the ashes after one of the fireplaces had been cleaned out, then race up and down the driveway."

He could picture her, pigtails flying, gap-toothed grin splitting her face while her mother stood in the doorway anxiously.

"I'll bet you were hell on wheels."

"A royal pain is more like it." Her engaging smile electrified him, made him forget what he was doing. A reaction that was one of the many reasons he had chosen to remain a bachelor.

It was the safe thing to do. The smart thing. Unlike his partner Danny, Lance would leave behind no widow or small child, no one to mourn when his number came up, as it surely would. Men in dangerous professions never expected to be around to draw social security.

"Is there anyplace around here where you'd get ashes on your wheels?"

"Nowhere except the backyard."

There were no signs that the little red wagon had come from that direction. That ruled out a thief who had sneaked through the backyard and inadvertently run through the debris from an O'Banyon fireplace.

"What kind of thief would pull a little red wagon, anyhow?" she said.

Jolie went up another notch in Lance's book. "That's the question I'm asking myself."

"And what answer did you come up with?"

"A Scrooge-like Santa who came down the chimney."

"Or a chimney sweep passing through town."

Jolie played his game without blinking an eye. Just like Danny. Pain as familiar as his right arm shot through Lance's heart, and he abandoned the game.

"The tracks go halfway down the drive...." He traced them to where they split to the left, while Jolie stayed close by. Too close. Lance veered to the right to put some distance between them. A cowardly thing to do. But that was his new modus operandi, wasn't it?

Headlines flashed through his mind. International Security Force Agent Dead... Flames Consume ISF Agent... ISF Agent Killed in Raid Gone Awry. Partner Lives.

Somebody had to take the blame, and the press

was all too eager to lay it at Lance's feet. "ISF Agent L. C. Estes stood by while his partner went up in flames. On a hot summer night in a small Italian village, Estes led a raid that cost his partner his life...."

"Lance?"

"Sorry. I was thinking...." Let her believe he was thinking about the Christmas thief. It was simpler that way.

"Well, look, thinking is much easier on a full stomach. Why don't we go inside and have a hearty breakfast, then go out and catch a thief?"

Visions of bacon sizzled a perfect golden brown and homemade biscuits light enough to float danced in his head.

"I can't tell you the last time I had a good home-cooked breakfast."

A funny look crossed her face, then she clapped him on the back and said, "Come on, then. What are we waiting for?"

Chapter Three

Collapsed biscuits charred in the oven and bacon burned in the pan while the most gorgeous man this side of heaven sat in the O'Banyon kitchen drinking coffee strong enough to float nails. It didn't help a bit that he was Elizabeth's boyfriend.

He belongs to Elizabeth…he belongs to Elizabeth. Jolie had to keep telling herself that.

She took a fortifying sip of coffee and nearly gagged. "I'm sorry I made the coffee a little strong."

"It's just the way I like it."

She added kindness to her long and ever-growing list of Lance Estes's assets. Kind men were usually tender. The very thought of Lance's tender hands ca-

ressing her melted Jolie right down to her knee pads.
A combination of wild and tender was so rare that
Jolie felt as if she'd found an exotic, practically ex-
tinct mountain cat. A gorgeous specimen not seen in
these parts since her ninth grade soccer coach moved
to Georgia and broke her teenaged heart.

"Maybe we ought to turn off the oven."

Lance's voice jerked her back to the ugly reality
of billowing smoke. She'd already set herself on fire
with forbidden desire. Next thing she knew she'd be
igniting her kitchen with flames that only Shady
Grove's volunteer fire department could extinguish.

Lance leaped from his chair, grabbed a hot pad
and jerked the smoking biscuits out of the oven. "Oh
dear," she said. What she'd strived for was the
fluffy, melt-in-your-mouth confection the recipe optimistically called "angel biscuits." What she got
was charcoal briquettes.

"Maybe I left out a vital ingredient," she said.

"Maybe." Was there no end to his generosity of
spirit?

"I'll try again." She was already dumping flour
in the bowl when he put a hand on her arm. Thoughts
of biscuits flew right out of her head.

"That's okay, Jolie. We can have cereal, or if you
don't have that, I can pick up some doughnuts in
town."

"We have plenty of cereal, but..." She pictured
cornflakes floating forlornly in skimmed milk, ac-

cusing her of failure with every soggy bite. "Oh, dear…"

"What's wrong? Are you all right?"

As long as he would keep touching her, she was more than all right; she was euphoric…and a dirty, low-down sister-betrayer. She moved to the refrigerator and poured two big glasses of orange juice.

"Sure, I'm fine." Did she dare risk handing him the glass? No, that meant touching again. Accidentally, of course. "We have all kinds of cereal. Take your pick."

Naturally, he chose the snap, crackle and pop kind, her personal favorite. Then he added lots of sugar, which was exactly the way she liked it.

"You don't happen to like lobster with butter, do you?" she said. Her favorite food on the face of the earth. Well, if you didn't count buttered popcorn.

"I can't get enough of it," he declared.

"That's what I was afraid of."

"I beg your pardon?"

"Elizabeth likes lobster," Jolie stated, and he looked at her as if she'd lost her mind. That's all she needed—another person who viewed her as the world's biggest bubblehead. "Where did you meet my sister?"

"Italy."

Jolie had been to Italy once, but not with a heart-throb. While Elizabeth strolled through moonlit pi-

azzas with her lover, Jolie had wrestled with weimaraners at an international dog show.

"I was there once," she said. "With a dog."

"I've been with a few of those myself."

"At least the four-legged ones know how to
heel."

Lance's laughter exploded throughout the kitchen,
and it was contagious. By the time they'd finished
wiping away tears of mirth, Jolie felt as if they were
becoming friends, which was a very good thing. He
might turn out to be her brother-in-law. Shoot, if
Elizabeth had a brain in head she would hang on to
Lance Estes.

"After we finish this sumptuous banquet cleverly
disguised as cereal, I'll be ready to help you catch a
thief," she said.

"You don't have to come along."

Didn't he want her? Probably not. Why would
anyone who loved her smart, successful sister want
to spend time with ditzy Jolie?

Still, it was *her* Christmas tree and *her* presents.
She had a right to tag along. Besides, the reinvented
Jolie needed to add keeping the family's gifts safe to
her new, responsible lifestyle.

"I want to," she said, and then, so he wouldn't
think she was stubborn, she added, "Besides, you
might need me to identify the Radio Flyer."

"Fine. Suit yourself."

She'd hoped for a more enthusiastic response, but

she tried not to take it personally. Besides, he redeemed himself by scrubbing the burned pan while she put their cereal bowls in the dishwasher.

"I never thought I'd see the bottom of that pan again," she said. "How'd you do that?"

"Elbow grease and experience."

"What kind of experience?"

"Growing up, I always got kitchen detail."

"We took turns around here, but since I was the youngest with the least forceful voice, I usually got the dirty jobs." She grabbed her baseball helmet and rammed it back on her head. Who knew what kind of trouble they'd encounter? And she wanted to be prepared. It was one of her new mottoes.

Lance looked as if he was holding back laughter, but what did she care? She wasn't out to impress her sister's boyfriend.

"Do you mind riding the motorcycle?" he said when they got outside.

"I'd love it!"

"Then you'll have to swap head gear." He handed her a small motorcycle helmet, obviously made for females, obviously worn by dozens of other women who couldn't resist that adorable dimple in his chin. Jolie reined herself in. Even if he weren't her sister's boyfriend, she had no intention of jumping into an ill-thought-out relationship. First she had to make some major changes within herself; she had to become somebody she could be proud of.

"Do you have a big family?" she asked as she climbed on behind him.

"No." He didn't offer further information, and she didn't ask. She was too busy trying to figure out the least dangerous spot for her hands.

"Just grab hold," he told her, and she did. She grabbed hold of the most gorgeous chest God had ever created, then tried her best to breathe.

Fortunately, she didn't have to do anything else for a very long time. They rode around Shady Grove at a snail's pace, searching for clues. She didn't know what Lance was looking for or even doing, for that matter, but she was scanning the streets for any sign of a little red wagon and trying to remain sane.

Around ten o'clock her cereal lost its snap, and by ten-thirty the crackle and pop had departed, as well. Obviously, Lance read minds, because he pulled over at Billy Jenkins's Pit Stop and All Purpose Store and said, "How about a snack?"

You could love a man who knew how to keep a woman well-fed. "Great. Billy has the best boiled peanuts in three counties."

"He does, huh?" Lance's light, teasing manner was almost like flirting, and she nearly let it go to her head. Fortunately, one of the new leaves she'd turned over was for common sense, not fantasy.

"Yep, he does. Follow me."

Lance bought a large bag of boiled peanuts, and they sat on the sagging picnic table underneath the store's only tree, a magnolia, Jolie's favorite. If she got her new job she hoped she wouldn't have to move where there were no magnolias.

"It is always this warm in December?" he asked.

"No. Sometimes we'll get a cold snap around late November, and once we even had a light dusting of snow for Christmas. Usually, though, you can count on a few balmy days this time of year. Our coldest weather will come in January and February."

She cracked a peanut and savored the warm, salty treat. "You're not from the South, are you?"

"No."

She waited—politely, she hoped—but he didn't reveal anything else, so she concentrated on her boiled peanuts and pretended she wasn't burning up with curiosity. Maybe she'd ask Elizabeth for his history.

Or maybe not. Especially since Jolie kept getting sidetracked by the way the sun turned his green eyes into deep pools.

Personally, she had always been a little fearful of plunging too deeply into a man's eyes. For one thing, men didn't take her seriously. For another, she'd found it easier to go along with the fiction that she was frivolous and carefree than put herself in a position where she might have to endure what her mother had. Not that Lucy O'Banyon Coltrane would ever admit she'd had a difficult marriage, and certainly not to her youngest child, but you didn't have to be a rocket scientist to feel the tension, listen to your mother crying behind closed doors and figure out that all was not perfect with the Coltranes.

Jolie was glad her mother had Dr. Ben now. It was good to see Lucy laughing again after all those years of playing the contented wife, then the grieving widow. Of course, her mother had an outlet: writing romance.

A talent for pretense was a skill Jolie had learned from Lucy's personal life and her professional one. Jolie wondered if her own life would have been different if she hadn't pretended to be something she was not. What would have happened if she'd finished college, gotten a *real* job, then selected a buttoned-down man and fallen straight into the depths of his steadfast eyes?

It was too late for that now. Her life was what it was, twenty-nine years of playing around in the shallows while everybody else she knew plunged into the deep waters and caught the big fish.

"Penny for your thoughts."

"I was thinking about wasted years and wasted potential."

Lord, what was there about Lance Estes that made her blurt out the truth?

He studied her a long time before he replied. "That's some mighty deep thinking."

"For such a shallow person, you mean." There she went again, speaking before she thought.

"No, I didn't."

"Surely Elizabeth told you about me."

"She said you love animals and take in strays. She didn't mention 'shallow' and she didn't say anything about your lethal aim."

Lance grinned at her, and how could Jolie help but smile back? After all, it was a beautiful day and it was almost Christmas…even if they didn't find the stolen gifts.

"Elizabeth is so lucky." She started to add *to have you,* but bit it back in time to save herself further embarrassment.

"All set?" he asked.

"Yes." She climbed aboard once more and tried to hold back her fantasies, but they refused to be banished. Well, why not dream? It was only natural to think romantic thoughts when you were squeezed up close to a dangerously sexy man in black leather. Wasn't it?

They scouted Main Street from one end to the other in fifteen minutes, and the entire town in less than an hour. The only suspicious person they saw was Mr. Leon Crumpett, who had obviously escaped the vigilance of his daughter and was fishing in the fountain in the town square in hip waders, with his grandson's baseball cap perched on his head like a mushroom.

Lance was coasting to a stop beside the fountain when Sgt. Wayne Gifford of the Shady Grove Police

Department took Mr. Crumpett by the arm and gently led him toward a waiting car.

"What's going on?" Lance asked Jolie.

"Wayne will take him back home. He's been a little *off* since his car accident six years ago. Everybody in town watches out for him."

"Good," Lance murmured. Then he said, "We've covered the town. What's on the outskirts?"

"Nothing but cotton and soybean fields and the town dump."

"Where's the dump?"

"We have to double back, then take Field Road."

Two miles out of town and another three down a potholed, blacktop road they came to Shady Grove's junkyard. It was surrounded by a chain-link fence with broken sections that nobody bothered to fix and a double gate nobody bothered to close, let alone lock.

They saw the little red wagon before they saw the thief. Dented and rusty, it sat among abandoned refrigerators and treadless tires and useless telephones...and it was piled high with Christmas packages wrapped in familiar paper.

Lance cut the engine. "Can you drive this thing?" he asked, and she nodded. "Good. Stay here. If I'm not back in ten minutes, go to the police."

"Okay."

She was not foolish. Danger lurked behind the carcasses of household appliances. Even with soccer pads, motorcycle helmet and a fearless heart, she didn't *really* know how to catch a thief. And she had no intention of becoming a target.

''Be careful,'' she whispered, but if Lance heard, he didn't give any indication. He was already blending with the landscape, a big man who had somehow vanished while she was looking at him.

She squinted her eyes, trying to catch a glimpse of him, but all she saw was a crow lifting off from the rusted-out hood of a 1973 Thunderbird convertible. Exactly who was Lance Estes, and how did he do that—vanish quietly without a trace?

Maybe she'd ask him. Or maybe not. If he were no more forthcoming about his profession than he'd been about his origins, she might as well save her breath. Shivers ran down her spine, in spite of her best intentions and recent resolutions. Mysterious men fascinated her, and Lance more than most.

What was he doing now? What was he finding? What time was it? Had ten minutes passed?

Jolie never wore a watch. They were a bother, always staying behind in places like hotel bathrooms and distant coliseums where she'd clipped, shampooed and groomed the world's champion dogs.

What if something had happened to Lance? What if the thief was a gun-toting madman who had already done him in and was at this very moment looking to do the same to Jolie?

She wasn't about to be caught unprepared. She slid

off the motorcycle and crept on hands and knees toward a pile of old tires and rusty pipes. Selecting a
pipe the size of a baseball bat that was only slightly
twisted on the end, she gave a practice swing and
decided she wouldn't go down easily.

Now that she was armed, shouldn't she go to
Lance's rescue? Shouldn't she at least look for him?

Crouched on the ground, torn between returning
to the relative safety of the motorcycle or wandering
among refrigerator carcasses, she jumped out of her
skin when Lance called her name.

Was he hurt? Dying? Trapped? Was it a warning
to run?

"Jolie," he called again. "Over here...the old yellow school bus."

Peering around the towering stack of tires, she
spotted it beyond a graveyard of vehicles.

"I'm coming." She jumped on the motorcycle,
started it up and wound her way through the junkyard
to the ancient, leaning bus. Most of its windows were
busted out and all the paint had peeled off except a
wide swath down one side, where a large oak tree
offered protection from the elements.

Lance appeared in the bus's doorway and, of all
things, he was smiling. What kind of thief made a
person smile?

"Come on in. I found our Christmas-loving visitor."

"Visitor?"

"You'll see. Brace yourself."

She did, but no amount of pulling up her mental bootstraps prepared Jolie for what lay just inside the bus. Everywhere she looked she saw O'Banyon Christmas ornaments in nests of pine needles, some on vacant seats, some carefully arranged on the driver's console. Some of the gifts had been unwrapped and placed about like little altars to the gods of innocence and unreason. Two diamond bracelets swinging from the rearview mirror caught the afternoon sun and shot rainbows across the bus. A tiny tiara Jolie had bought for Matt's little girl glittered from the rusty old ceiling, suspended there by a length of gold satin ribbon Jolie had used to tie the package. The books the O'Banyons and Coltranes were fond of giving each other teetered in a tower formation at the back of the bus, and on top of them sat a nest woven of multicolored Christmas ribbon.

In the midst of it all stood a birdlike woman in a dusty pink chenille robe, high-topped running shoes with the laces untied, and leftover ribbon woven in her abundant gray hair.

Lance bowed to the little woman, then took her hand and led her toward Jolie as if she were a queen. "Jolie, I want you to meet the Bird Lady."

Chapter Four

Jolie reached out and smiled as if she were shaking hands with the mayor's wife instead of holding the dirty hand of a stranger who had squirreled away stolen gifts.

"I'm so pleased to meet you," Jolie said.

Nothing escaped Lance's observation. Not the tenderness of Jolie's smile nor the sincerity in her voice. Not the way compassion bloomed across her face nor the way she held on to the Bird Lady with one hand and patted her with the other.

"Shh," the old woman said. "You'll wake up the baby birds." Jolie gave Lance a quizzical look, and he nodded toward the ornaments in their makeshift nests. "They're about to hatch."

"I see." Jolie spoke without a hint of amusement, which raised Lance's estimation of her another notch.

"I found them," the woman murmured.

"You did?"

"In a great big house on the hill. The mother flew off and they were waiting for me."

"I told her we'd help take care of them," Lance said. "Unless you have other ideas."

Most women would have weighed all the options, or motioned him outside and said, *What do you mean, take care of them? I'm calling the police.* But not the unflappable Jolie Kat Coltrane in her impossibly endearing flak gear and her long braid.

"Of course we will." She tossed him the keys to the motorcycle. "I'll stay with her while you go get the car."

"You're sure?"

"Positive. What the O'Banyon Manor needs is more baby birds about to hatch and the Bird Lady to watch over them."

She turned to the little woman. "It's supposed to turn cold tonight. You don't mind if we move them to a warmer place, do you?"

"No. As long you're careful."

"We will be. I promise."

Lance had no doubt that Jolie would be safe, but still he said, "You're sure about this?"

"Absolutely."

"All right then. I'll be back in less than thirty minutes. I don't think you'll have any trouble."

"Of course we won't. We have lots to talk about. Oh, and Lance, why don't you bring back a big box from the kitchen pantry. We'll need it for the baby birds."

The Bird Lady lost interest in their conversation and began to sway to music no one else could hear.

Jolie got tears in her eyes. "The sweet dear," she whispered.

"Nobody to dance with," the Bird Lady said, and Jolie shoved aside the books to waltz her slowly up and down the aisles.

Lance left them dancing in the cramped bus, with an ache in his empty heart and the nagging fear that he had let the best things in life pass him by.

Though O'Banyon Manor was less than ten minutes away, it took them an hour to get the Bird Lady and her nests loaded into the car and transported back there. They'd all had a late lunch of ham and cheese sandwiches—the elderly woman ate two—and now, while Jolie supervised the Bird Lady's bath, Lance sat in the library making calls to the area's hospitals and nursing homes to find out who she was.

Laughter floated down the stairs, Jolie's full-bodied, no-holds-barred glee and the Bird Lady's bell-like peals of mirth. He found himself grinning for no reason at all. When he stopped to think about it, he realized he'd laughed more in the past two days than he had in the last two years.

It felt good, heartwarming and soul-satisfying in ways he'd never dreamed. Of course, he tried very hard *not* to dream, but he was rediscovering the urge, teetering on the edge of some forgotten place within himself.

The voice of the supervisor at Langston Nursing Home came to him over the receiver: "I'm sorry. We have no one here who fits that description. All our residents are accounted for."

That was the last nursing home in Lee County. Could the Bird Lady be like him? Homeless. No known identity... He was swept back into the past, into the hot desert country of the Southwest, where he'd been found on the steps of the orphanage in a handwoven, Native American blanket.

There was no note telling us your name so we called you Lancelot, because your cries were like a warrior. That's what the first housemother, Ina Estes, had told him, a kind soul who was at the orphanage until she'd married and moved away. He'd been five years old, and heartbroken to see her leave.

He'd selected his last name himself. When he was old enough he'd legally changed the name Smith, which the orphanage had given him, to Estes in honor of the only mother he'd ever known.

He didn't think she'd mind, although clearly at

least half his blood was Native American. His deep olive skin, thick black hair and high cheekbones gave that away.

He'd tried his best to honor her name, and had, too, until that hot summer in Italy....

"Lance?" Jolie stood in the doorway with a woman he would hardly have recognized if he hadn't known she was the only little old lady in the house. "What do you think?"

The Bird Lady wore khaki slacks and a bright pink blouse that put color in her cheeks and emphasized her dark eyes. Instead of scruffy, high-topped tennis shoes, she now wore a tiny pair of red Western boots.

Lance took the little lady's fragile hands and said, "You look great."

"Got on my dancing boots." She stuck one foot out for his inspection.

"I let her pick out her own shoes." Jolie turned to the old lady. "In fact, they *are* dancing shoes. I used to wear them to a club in Nashville."

"And my ribbons." The Bird Lady patted her hair. "Do you like my ribbons?"

Head cocked like an inquisitive sparrow, she peered up at him and his heart melted. "I like the ribbons very much. They're cheerful, and they match your boots."

The Bird Lady was there, and then suddenly she wasn't. Rocking back and forth on her boots, humming, she simply disappeared into her own world.

Motioning for Jolie to follow, Lance moved to the French doors so they would be out of hearing. "I haven't found out who she is or where she belongs."

A hint of moisture glistened in Jolie's eyes. "That's so sad."

"If she ran away from her family, this could take a while. I've called the hospital, and all the nursing homes in Lee County. It's too late to call nursing homes outside the county. I'll do that tomorrow."

Jolie turned to study their visitor, who was dancing again with a faraway expression in her eyes. "Just look at her. She seems as if she doesn't have a care in the world."

"Compensation. When the mind goes, so do the cares."

"Just think how awful it would be to be left all alone in the world with nobody to buy you a new dress or remember you with a gift. Especially at Christmas." Jolie wiped her eyes on the edge of her sleeve. "Don't you think somebody would have sounded the alarm by now?"

"She could be one of the forgotten old. Their numbers are legion."

"As long as she's here she's not forgotten. O'Banyon Manor is her home until we can locate her real one."

The Bird Lady twirled toward them, then looked at Lance and stopped. "Jacky?" Standing on tiptoe, she cupped his face. "Are you my Jacky?"

"Who is Jacky?"

Confusion contorted her face. "He was in first grade and then...." She clapped her hand over her mouth and twirled off.

"Do you think she has a son?" Jolie asked.

"Could be."

"Oh...just look at her."

Standing beside one of the bird's nests, the Bird Lady stroked a bright blue Christmas ball and crooned, "There, there, baby birdie, I'll take good care of you." Looking up, she said, "Jacky, come see. It's a songbird."

Her request tugged at his heart in ways Lance didn't want to think about. Under any other circumstances he'd have set the woman straight, then walked away. But it was almost Christmas. What would it hurt to play along with an old lady's fantasy?

"Pet him, Jacky," she said, and Lance didn't even feel foolish as he rubbed the blue glass ornament. What he felt was some long-buried tenderness and a thawing around his heart.

The Bird Lady rested her hand on his arm, swaying a little. "It's the bluebird of happiness," she whispered.

And he answered, "Yes, it is."

"I'd like to sleep now."

She was leaning heavily on him, and Lance picked her up and said, "I'll tuck you in."

"Can you carry her up the stairs?" Jolie said.

"Yes. She weighs no more than a baby bird herself."

"Follow me."

Jolie led him to a room with a rose-printed comforter and ruffles. Lance deposited the Bird Lady in a nest of pillows on the four-poster bed, then secured the windows.

"We'll lock the door," he said. "That way we can be certain she won't run away."

"Oh, no. What if she wakes up and gets scared? I'll stay here and watch her."

"She might sleep till morning."

"That's all right." Jolie tugged off the cowboy boots and spread the quilt over the sleeping Bird Lady. "I'll grab a book and something to eat. I'll be fine." She worried her lower lip. "Of course, that leaves you hanging around with nothing to do."

"Don't worry. I had expected to be here alone, anyway." Seeing her crestfallen look, he added, "Having your company is a bonus I hadn't counted on."

Her glowing smile was his reward. "Okay, then. Will you watch her a minute while I go fetch my stuff?"

"Sure thing."

Within fifteen minutes Jolie came back with one of her mother's romance novels—steamy, if the cover was any indication—and an armload of junk food. All she lacked to withstand a siege was her makeshift flak gear.

"All set," she said. "I hope you don't mind being on your own."

"Not at all."

"The library is filled with books, the bubble is over the swimming pool in case you want to swim, the exercise room is in the basement and the kitchen is full of sandwich stuff. I'll be right here." She smiled. "Oh, and in case you want to call Elizabeth or something, don't hesitate to use the phone."

"I have my cell."

"Well, naturally, but sometimes the signal gets messed up here. Shady Grove is not the center of the universe, popular opinion to the contrary."

Jolie made it so easy to smile. "I'll bear that in mind."

He was at the door when she called him back. "You're sure you'll be okay by yourself?"

"I've been taking care of myself for a very long time." *All my life*, he thought, though Jolie's concern for his welfare touched him deeply. "Thanks, anyway."

She unwrapped a candy bar and held it out. "Have a bite?"

"No, thanks." Lance escaped. And just in the nick of time, for Jolie's chocolate had gone soft and the bite she took left an endearing smear at the corner of her mouth. Besides that, she was making delicious humming sounds, and though he knew it was merely contentment over a candy bar, he had visions of another kind—Jolie in bed approaching the act of intimacy the way she did everything else, full speed ahead, no holds barred.

The swimming pool provided some relief, then afterward he worked himself into a lather on the rowing machine in the basement. No sense going soft while he was in Mississippi. Soft bodies could get a man killed.

What about soft hearts?

A vision of Jolie hovering over a homeless woman came to him, but Lance pushed it firmly aside. He had no intention of being seduced into letting down his guard.

Instead he called Elizabeth.

"Just wanted to let you know I'm here," he told her.

"Great. I'm sorry my kid sister's there. I know how much you were looking forward to a week of peace and solitude."

"No, everything's fine."

"Kat means well, but she can be…scatterbrained at times. Just tell her no if she tries to rope you into one of her escapades."

Let it go, he told himself. It would be the easy thing, but taking the easy way out was not his style. And besides, he couldn't get that smear of chocolate out of his mind.

"Actually, I'm enjoying her company."

"Really?"

"Yes. She's a delightful young woman."

"I'm glad you like her."

"Yeah, she's a great kid." Though Elizabeth was one of the most levelheaded, feet-firmly-planted women he'd ever met, he didn't want her getting ideas. "If the rest of your family is as nice as she is, this will be a memorable Christmas."

"They are. Eccentric, but lovable. I hate to cut this short, Lance, but they're yelling for me on the set."

After he'd hung up, Lance sat in the gathering darkness thinking about twists of fate, about how a chance encounter at a small café in Italy had led him to the lovely, self-possessed woman who almost made him believe in himself again.

He'd met Elizabeth Coltrane shortly after the accident that had claimed Danny's life. She was warm and beautiful, intelligent and easy to talk to, and he met her at a time when he needed to talk, when he was under fire from every major newspaper in the world, as well as his own conscience. Could he have saved his partner? Had he made major mistakes in the planning stages of the operation? Was he losing his edge? Those were the questions he'd asked himself.

Now, alone in the library, he listened to the quiet voice of the mansion, not a silence but an echo of Coltrane and O'Banyon voices, years of family history contained within the bricks and mortar Jolie Kat Coltrane called home.

A great sense of loss descended on him, and with it a longing so fierce he almost groaned aloud. Lance had no history and no place to call home. Not really. Except for his state-of-the-art kitchen, the apartment he kept in Atlanta was functional at best, a roof over his head, someplace to hang his hat between assignments.

He thought of Jolie upstairs curled into a chintz-covered chair with chocolate on her mouth, immersed in her book. Was she dreaming of romance? Of falling in love? Of a life that included happily ever after?

Who would the lucky guy be? Somebody she already knew? Somebody with parents and grandparents and a long, illustrious list of ancestors that went all the way back to the eighteenth century?

Lance stalked into the kitchen and snapped on the light. Jolie's future was none of his business...but her immediate comfort was. There was no need for her to sit upstairs ruining her health on junk food when he was perfectly capable of providing a nutritious meal.

He would continue the search for the Bird Lady's home tomorrow. Tonight he had another mission: making a pot of soup.

Chapter Five

Jolie crumpled the empty potato chip bag and tossed it into the wastebasket, then tiptoed to the bed to check on the Bird Lady. She was still sleeping, and if the deep sound of her breathing was any indication, she was out until tomorrow.

It was only nine o'clock. Jolie was in for a long night. As she walked around the room to stretch her cramped legs she wished for her nightshirt, her robe and another glass of Coke. Wasn't it just like her to get stuck without all the things necessary for comfort? If she wanted to make real changes in her life, she'd better start being prepared.

Elizabeth never forgot anything. She noted everything in her day planner with copious sticky notes in bright colors coordinated according to the importance of the task: hot pink for *urgent,* yellow for *sometime today,* blue for *when you can.*

Personally, Jolie thought the sticky notes went a little too far, but first thing tomorrow she was going to buy herself a day planner...after she'd made a follow-up call to the SPCA about her job.

Feeling better now that she'd made strides toward self-improvement, she picked up the candy wrapper and licked away the last remaining bits of chocolate, then turned to page 150 in her mother's romance novel.

She was the only one of her siblings who actually enjoyed their mother's books, though Jolie knew for a fact that Matt had read a few when he was courting Sandi. Her sister-in-law had told her.

Elizabeth had read the first one and told Lucy how proud she was, but she didn't have time to read the rest of them—fifty-something in all.

Jolie supposed most folks would look at her mother's massive bibliography as the outpouring of a prolific writer, but she saw the array of novels in a different light: the fruits of a lonely woman.

Of course, when you considered that Lucy was happy now and still wrote just as many romances, Jolie's logic didn't hold up. Nothing new there. On a scale of one to ten, her logic skills ranked about two.

She was giggling over one of her mother's co-medic scenes when the door opened and in wafted the most delicious smell this side of heaven. Right behind the divine fragrance came Lance bearing a tray with three steaming bowls, two glasses of wine and a glass of tea.

"I thought you might be hungry."

"Hungry? I'm starving. What smells so deli-cious?"

"Macadamia nut soup."

"Wow. Where on earth did you find it? Mother didn't tell me Shady Grove had opened a gourmet restaurant."

"They haven't. As far as I know." He set the tray on the table beside her chair. "I made it."

"You *made* it?" *Drat.* Wasn't it just like Elizabeth to fall for the perfect man? Leather jacket, tender ways, good looks and a great cook to boot. Jolie could get depressed if she'd let herself.

"Cooking is a hobby. It beats movie violence pos-ing as entertainment."

"I enjoy a good blood-and-guts flick myself," she said, and he smiled at her the way an indulgent par-ent would a wayward child.

"I see the Bird Lady is still sleeping."

"Yes. I haven't heard a peep. I guess she's ex-hausted after scrounging for herself for so long."

"Not to mention breaking and entering."

While he pulled up the only other chair in the

room, Jolie noted the linen napkins and the crystal vase with its single rose, obviously from the Don Juan climber in the rose garden. "This is mighty fancy," she said.

"You deserve it," Lance answered simply.

Her head grew about two sizes too big for her soccer helmet...if she'd been wearing it. In fact, the remark so flattered her and inspired her to fantasy that she forgot the soup.

"I'll go down and fix you a sandwich if you'd like," Lance said.

"No...oh, no. I *love* soup." Good grief, she sounded like a simpering teen or else one of those women who batted her eyelashes and talked as if she had a mouth full of butter and honey. "At least I *think* I do."

She dipped her spoon in and closed her eyes as she took a bite. With the next she rolled her eyes. And on the third she groaned as if she were in the throes of ecstasy. Which she was.

Lance smiled. "That's the best endorsement my cooking's ever had."

Jolie took another bite. "Oh, my Lord, how did you *make* this?"

"With a little chicken broth, a few scallions, ground macadamia nuts and lots of cream added at the last minute."

"No, I mean...practically anybody can read recipes. It takes a special skill to make them turn out right."

"I take it you were cooking last night."

She giggled. "Trying."

His smile caught her unaware. It was glorious, starting at his eyes and spreading all over his face. And the way he was staring at her... It was enough to make her believe in impossible dreams.

"Jolie…"

"Hmm?"

"There's something I have to tell you."

Here it comes. He's going to say he's engaged to Elizabeth.

"Elizabeth and I…"

"I know. And believe me, I'm happy for you, I really am."

"She told you?"

"Well, no, but it wouldn't take a rocket scientist to figure it out. I mean, she's beautiful and smart and successful and here you are…."

Jolie ran out of steam. All of a sudden she was so dejected she didn't even want the world's best soup.

"Here I am…what?"

"Well, for Pete's sake. Look at yourself. You're the world's most gorgeous man, plus you have a heart the size of Texas and a noble streak as big as Kansas. Why wouldn't Elizabeth fall for you?"

"Elizabeth and I are *friends*."

"What are you saying? You broke up?"

"We were never together. We met in Italy, and she was kind to me when I needed a friend. I shouldn't have let you run on the way you did, but every now and then a man likes to hear flattering remarks from a lovely woman."

Everything vanished in a swirl—the soup, the room, the dear little lady on the bed, the remains of Jolie's junk food binge. There was nothing left except her and the man who thought she was lovely.

"Really?"

"Yes. Most men won't admit it, but we love having our egos stroked."

"I mean, do you really think I'm lovely?"

"Yes." That smile again. She reveled in it, bathed in it, got lost in it. Then ever so slowly Lance leaned toward her, and she got so nervous and excited she nearly fell off her chair.

He was going to kiss her. She could see it coming, feel it, taste it. She was actually getting ready to pucker up when he rubbed the side of her mouth with his thumb.

"You have chocolate here." Oh, Lord, his hand on her face felt wonderful, miraculous. She wished she had chocolate from head to toe.

Keep doing it, she thought, and mercifully, he did.

"Right there," he murmured, while his gentle touch turned her into a new woman. Somebody altogether different from cute, funny Kat Coltrane. She became scintillating, mysterious, glamorous…and totally off her rocker.

Pulling back from paradise, she wiped her mouth with her napkin. "Thanks."

"You're welcome," he answered calmly, then went on eating his soup. Naturally, he would. He was cleaning up her messy face, that was all. He hadn't meant to set her imagination on fire and heat up her blood. He certainly hadn't meant to kiss her.

And she was glad, she really was. She intended to put out the fire as quickly as possible, probably as soon as he left the room and she could breathe again. Jolie Kat Coltrane was busy becoming a new woman. She absolutely, positively did not have time to get sidetracked by a dangerously attractive man.

Instead she finished her soup…then gazed with longing at the extra bowl.

"Here." Lance handed it to her. "I don't think Birdie is going to wake up."

"I was thinking the same thing myself." Jolie had her spoon already poised over the bowl when she remembered her manners. "Are you sure you don't want it?"

"Positive. There's a potful in the kitchen."

"Oh, goodie."

Lance looked like a man holding back laughter, and then he simply let it go.

"What?" she said.

"You."

"I know. I'm silly."

"No. Delightful. At times a little girl and other times…" He didn't finish the sentence. Instead he went to the bed and bent over the Bird Lady. When he sat back down he had the closed-up look of a man with secrets.

"Do you think she's all right?" Jolie asked.

"Yes. She appears to be sleeping normally. I'll stay with her the rest of the night."

"There's no need."

"You look all tuckered out."

"I'll admit it has been a long day. But of course, you had the same long day."

"I'm used to it."

"Why?"

"Part of the job."

She would have pursued the subject of his job but his look warned her away. Puzzled and saddened, Jolie wondered how she could have gone from lovely to outcast in the space of fifteen minutes.

It was just as well, for in spite of her staunch resolutions, she was having a hard time reining in her wild imagination and her stampeding heart.

"That's very kind of you, but you don't have to stay. Really." After all, wasn't he the one who had suggested they lock the door?

"I'll stay. You go to bed."

The look he gave her brooked no argument, and truth to tell, she was glad to escape.

"I'll take the dishes on my way out." She picked up the tray, waiting. For what, she didn't know. Maybe for him to say *Don't go. Stay.*

Instead he said, "Good night, Jolie. Sleep tight."

It wasn't *Sweet dreams,* but at least it was something.

In the kitchen she rinsed the bowls and started loading the dishwasher, but the call of gourmet soup lured her over to the stewpot.

She lifted the lid and there it was—five thousand calories per bite, the best soup she'd ever tasted, prepared by the world's most delicious man.

Sighing, Jolie ladled out another portion. "I don't care if it makes me fat," she said. Then she put her bowl on the cooking island and ate the soup standing up. Just on general principle.

Chapter Six

It was perfectly natural for Jolie to wake up in a houseful of people, even complete strangers, for often her mother or Aunt Kitty and even Dolly Wilder, would invite someone to visit O'Banyon Manor. And often as not the guests ended up staying longer than they intended because they loved the quiet beauty of the northeast Mississippi hills and the warm hospitality of their hostesses.

So there was nothing new about walking into her kitchen and seeing the Bird Lady perched on a bar stool or Lance lounging against the counter with a cup of coffee. The unusual thing was that a guest had prepared the food.

Jolie's nose led her to a vast array of delicacies lined up in front of the Bird Lady: sausages and eggs and bacon, waffles cooked to a golden perfection that made her mouth water.

"Good morning," Lance said. "Did you sleep well?"

"Yes. But I always do. The sleep of the innocent, Elizabeth calls it. She's an insomniac."

"I made breakfast."

"No, you made a feast. My goodness, how did you do that?"

"With a great cheering section. We got up very early and I cooked while she had macadamia nut soup."

"The songbird didn't hatch," the Bird Lady said, then added another sausage to her plate, poured syrup on it and happily forgot all about her birds.

Jolie filled her own plate, choosing a little bit of everything. "If I could cook like this I'd weigh a ton. Why don't you?"

"I rarely get a chance to cook."

"Why not?"

"I travel a lot. It's part of my job." Before she could ask more, Lance changed the subject. "I found out who our guest is. They call her Birdie, and she's a resident at Hanging Grapes Haven."

"But that's in another county. How did she come so far? And with that little red wagon?"

"The director says Birdie is very clever at escaping and hitchhiking. Every time she's brought back, whether it's December or May, she tells them she's been looking for Christmas. In fact, she's been caught near here before.''

''So our tree drew her.... Doesn't she have family to watch out for her, to take her home on the holidays?''

''No.''

Her plate forgotten, Jolie said, ''Oh, I think I'm going to cry.'' Naturally, she didn't have a tissue. Which turned out to be a wonderful thing, because Lance cupped her face and wiped her tears away with his fingertips.

''Don't cry, Jolie. I can't bear seeing you in tears.''

A girl could build a whole future around moments like this...if she wasn't trying so hard to be practical.

''Do we have to take her back right away?'' she asked. ''I'd like to get her some clothes and some Christmas presents. Surprises. Frivolous baubles she can set around her room.''

''I'll see what I can do,'' he said. Just like that, he made her feel pampered, as if her every wish was his command.

She watched while he made the call, then when he said, ''Thanks, we'll bring her home this evening,'' Jolie threw her arms around him. And for a lovely moment, he hugged her back.

Then he gently disengaged himself. "Where would you like to go first?"

"I didn't think men liked to shop."

"Who told you that?"

"Well, I don't know. I guess I just assumed."

"Don't ever assume anything, Jolie."

He didn't add *especially about me,* but Jolie got the distinct feeling that's what he meant. If Lance Estes was anything, he was a man of mystery.

Plus a fabulous cook. How come some people—such as Elizabeth and Matt and Lance—had so many talents and others—such as Jolie—had so little?

Well, that wasn't exactly true. She was a darn good ball player, and nobody could clip and groom poodles the way she could. But she was thinking about *real* talent, the kind that counted for something.

"Why the long face, Jolie?"

"Oh, nothing."

Lance let it slide, and Jolie was glad. Self-analysis and self-improvement were wearing her out. Besides, she absolutely, positively was not going to fall in love with a man who didn't love her back.

She gave Lance and Birdie her best Jolie's-having-a-great-day smile, then said, "Who's ready to have some fun?"

Birdie raised her hand like a little kid in second grade, and Lance smiled. Jolie wasn't about to let a smile sidetrack her.

She had an agenda, and this time she was deter-mined to stick to it, come hell or high water.

"Okay, then, let's do it."

With Lance's help—a girl could get used to that—she made quick work of the dishes; then they climbed into the car and drove to the new gift shop in Shady Grove. Jolie hadn't been in yet, but she loved the name, My Favorite Things.

The Bird Lady went straight to the wind chimes. "Music," she exclaimed, then set every one of the chimes to tinkling.

"I think I know what I'm going to get her for Christmas," Jolie told Lance. "If they don't cost an arm and a leg."

The living she made was modest by any standards, and her last trip had just about cleaned her out. What little she had saved she planned to use to further her education.

When she looked at the price tag her face fell. Wouldn't you know it? Sixty dollars. What had hap-pened to shops that sold items for ten dollars or less? How could wind chimes cost so much?

She turned the tag over. "Tuned," it stated. She'd gladly have settled for an out-of-tune chime, but Birdie was standing there enchanted and hopeful. Jo-lie could cut a few corners. When she got back to Memphis she might even find a cheaper apartment, something without a view of the river. Who needed to see the river? And who was she to complain when she had so much and Birdie had so little?

Jolie started digging around in her purse. Naturally, her credit card was hiding. Now where had she put it? As soon as she got home she was going to add "buy a credit card wallet" to her list. Elizabeth had one made of real Italian leather. Jolie had seen some nice five-dollar knockoffs at the flea market in Memphis.

"Jolie." Lance put his hand on her shoulder. "You don't need your credit card. The salesclerk has mine. Put anything you want on it."

"Good grief. I can't let you do that."

"In view of your family's generous hospitality, it's the least I can do."

She grinned at him. "Yes, Virginia, there is a Santa Claus...."

Oh, help. She wanted to kiss him right in the middle of downtown Shady Grove, and from the look in his eyes, he wanted to kiss her right back. Or was it just wishful thinking on her part?

"Thanks," she whispered.

"You're welcome. More than welcome. You're..." His eyes held hers for another small eternity, and then he walked away.

Sighing, Jolie selected a wind chime, then followed him and Birdie to a sparkling display of stained glass. The one that caught her eye featured a red bird among green leaves.

Jolie picked it up. "Do you suppose her room at the nursing home has a window?"

"If it doesn't, I'll get her moved to one that does," Lance murmured.

"You can do that?"

"I can try."

"A man like you could come in handy. Why hasn't some woman snatched you up?"

"Just lucky, I guess."

Now what in the heck did he mean by that? That he was lucky, or the woman?

Jolie wasn't about to ask. For someone dedicated to making herself over, she was far too interested in this man.

He could clean like a demon and cook like a dream, and he was generous besides. Maybe if she looked hard enough she'd find something awful about him, something that would turn her mind away from fantasies and back toward her goals.

"Let's get all of these with birds," Lance said. In addition to the cardinal, there was a bluebird, a canary, a mockingbird and a finch. He plucked them off the display, and when he held them up, the sun reflected through the prisms. "She can have rainbows, too."

Jolie's heart did a flip-flop. Oh help, she was fixing to do something rash and foolish again. If she didn't take some drastic evasive action, she was going to fall in love.

"That's nice. I think I'll go over here and look at CDs. My old CD player is still at O'Banyon Manor, and I'm going to give it to Birdie." She said this as casually as possible, then strolled away. It was hard to act nonchalant when your skin was flushed and your chest felt like a boom box.

Putting her hand over her heart and breathing deeply, Jolie stood in front of the display of CDs for three minutes before she could make out the titles.

One more deep breath. She was in the blues section, and she had enough cash in her purse to get the John Lee Hooker CD she was sure Birdie would like.

The back of her neck prickled. Shoot, her whole body prickled. She could feel Lance off to her right, watching her. Lord, some men generated body heat, but he generated lightning bolts. With her breath coming in ragged spurts, she snatched up the CD and marched to the cash register.

"I'll take this," she said, then plopped down her cash.

Lance stood behind her with an armload of CDs. "Add these to my bill," he told the clerk, who positively beamed at him.

Wouldn't you know she was a dark-haired beauty with a perfect complexion and a beautiful smile? Why *wouldn't* she flirt with the best-looking man in Shady Grove?

And how come her flirtatious manner made Jolie want to spit ten-penny nails?

"I think we should move on," she said.

"To another store?"

Darn his hide. Why did he have to *smirk?*

"Yes. We need to get Birdie some clothes."

Jolie made a magnificent exit. The only downside was that she left Birdie in the store. Swallowing her pride, she went back inside, where she found the Bird Lady patting Lance's arm and calling him Jacky.

"I've already put my package in the car," Jolie said. Lame excuse.

"Great. If you'll hang on to Birdie, I'll stash the rest."

By the time Lance got the car loaded, Jolie had forgotten her pique with the flirtatious salesclerk and regained her Christmas spirit. Feeling festive and generous-hearted, she turned on the radio and sang along with Elvis, who was crooning "Blue Christmas" in his inimitable voice.

To her surprise, Lance joined in, while Birdie clapped and added a few doo-wahs.

"Hey, you're not a half-bad Elivis," Jolie told him after the song had ended.

"Neither are you."

"Yeah, but I don't have the sideburns."

"Neither do I."

"But you can grow them and I can't."

"Thank God. It would ruin that pretty little face of yours."

Jolie's spirits got so puffed up the entire town took

on a sparkle she had never noticed before. Even the ordinary green awnings over Martha's Boutique looked festive.

"Birdie's new wardrobe is on the Coltranes," she told Lance.

"I'm more than happy to pay."

"Mother will be, too, when I tell her I used her charge account for a very good cause."

Lance had never figured he'd enjoy shopping in a women's boutique. But as he sat near the dressing rooms on a pink satin boudoir chair about three sizes too small for his big frame, and watched Jolie's delight at outfitting the Bird Lady, he realized he hadn't stopped smiling in the last hour.

"What do you think about this one?" she said, holding up a bright red dress, and he said the same thing he had the last five times she'd asked: "It's great."

"Really?"

"Absolutely."

He didn't know the first thing about fashion, particularly women's fashion; he was simply taking his cues from Jolie's face. Observing her from his uncomfortable perch—his bottom was dangerously close to the floor, his knees nearly up to his chin— he could tell when she believed she had unearthed a treasure.

If he'd known it was this easy and this much fun to make a woman happy....

Whoa, boy! That kind of thinking's dangerous.

But he wouldn't have done a thing differently, Lance told himself firmly. Today he was doing a good deed for a sweet homeless lady, that was all.

Oh, yeah? Then why is your undivided attention on Jolie?

He was losing his perspective. That's what came of being in the bosom of a Southern family. Well, the rest of the family would be there soon, he reminded himself. Too much Southern hospitality was making him sentimental.

"Look at this one!" Cheeks flushed and eyes glowing, Jolie paraded by with a blouse the color of a bluebird's egg. "Don't you just love it?"

"To tell the truth, I don't know much about dresses." He unfolded himself from the chair. "I need to go outside and stretch my legs."

"Okay. We'll be finished in a minute."

"Take your time."

She stood on tiptoe and kissed him lightly on the cheek. "You're a sweetie pie."

A sweetie pie?

Nobody had ever called him anything endearing, let alone sweet. Pet names were for babies and old ladies and fools in love.

Then why did he like it? God, he needed fresh air

more than he'd thought. He all but ran from the boutique.

As the day had progressed, it had warmed up. That was the Deep South for you, even in December. However, there was still enough breeze to fan his hot face. He gulped air like a runner who had just completed a marathon.

Sweetie pie!

The next thing he knew he'd be looking around for a drive-in movie, then asking Jolie out just for the privilege of sitting in the car with her hips close to his and her face shiny with moonlight.

Damn.

He had to do something, and fast. He glanced through the window long enough to see that she was still avidly going through the racks, then he stalked down the street. He needed physical activity. He needed air. He needed a brain transplant.

"Lance." He heard Jolie's voice, then her footsteps, and the scent of her perfume reached him.

He stood on the sidewalk with his heart on his sleeve, feeling just like a teenager. Like a besotted fool who didn't know better than to stand around gazing at her pretty, flushed face and wanting to run his fingers through her thick, tousled hair.

"Is something wrong?" she asked.

"No. Why?"

"You look disgruntled."

"I'm not disgruntled."

"You're sure?"

"Positive." Her cheerful smile faded, and he was instantly contrite. "It's okay. Really. I'm used to lots of physical activity. That's all."

"Okay." Her smile came back. Thank heavens. "I just came to tell you Birdie is trying on her last dress, and then we're ready to go."

"Where to?"

"What time is it?"

"Two o'clock."

"I suppose we should go home so we can eat lunch, and I can wrap Birdie's Christmas gifts." Jolie drew a deep breath. "And then I guess we have to take her back."

He wanted to cup her face and kiss her softly, then say, "Everything's going to be okay." Instead he rammed his hands into his pockets to prevent involuntary acts of soft-hearted nonsense.

"I'll load the packages," he said.

Chapter Seven

After a lunch where Birdie ate the rest of the soup plus a ham sandwich, and Jolie ate hardly a bite, they loaded the car and headed toward the nursing home in Pontotoc. It was called Hanging Grapes Haven.

When Lance commented on the strange name, Jolie told him, "The Chickasaw Indian name for Pontotoc was Land of the Hanging Grapes."

She barely got this out without bursting into tears. What would happen to the Bird Lady after they left her off? Would she run away again? Would anybody search for her? What if somebody awful found her?

Jolie parked the car and then just sat there gripping the wheel.

"Jolie…" Lance touched her arm, then quickly withdrew his hand. "I know how you feel."

"You do?"

"Yes. I feel the same way. I'm going to have a talk with the director."

She nodded. "Put my name down as someone to contact on her behalf. Even after I go back to Memphis, I'm only an hour and a half away." She jotted her address and phone number on the back of a blank check, and made a mental note to add "notepad for purse" to her list.

"You're a good person, Jolie Kat Coltrane."

She smiled. "So are you, Lance Estes."

When they helped Birdie out of the car, the old woman put her hand on Lance's arm and said, "Are we home, Jacky?"

"We're home, Birdie."

Jolie swallowed hard, then followed a nurse's aid to Birdie's room, while Lance went into the office of the director to straighten things out. The room wasn't bad by nursing home standards, holding a bed, a nightstand with a cheap lamp, two chairs, and a small chest with a mirror above it. Everything was clean and neat. And depressingly uninviting. The room looked as if nobody lived there. There were no flowers, no pictures, no rugs, no cozy afghans.

Birdie stood in the middle of the room looking forlorn.

"Let's get you settled," Jolie told her, but the elderly woman didn't move, just stood there gazing out the window.

"You know what this room needs? Your baby birds." Jolie reached into one of the bags and brought out the Christmas ornaments in their make-shift nests.

"My birds!"

"Yes. Where do you want to put them?"

Birdie fluttered around the room, placing ribbon nests on the windowsill, on the chest, on the night-stand. While she sat on the edge of her bed caressing a bright red Christmas ball, Jolie hung the sun catchers in the window, plugged in the stereo and put on a Christmas CD—Nat King Cole singing "The Christmas Song"—and hung the wind chimes above the vent so the draft would set them tinkling.

In addition to her stereo, she had brought a table-top tree she'd found in the attic. It had twinkling colored lights and miniature ornaments in the shape of Frosty and Santa Claus and the Snow Fairy. When Jolie was six she'd thought it was the most wonderful tree in the world.

As soon as she plugged it in, Birdie clapped her hands and began to dance.

"It's Christmas," she said, and Jolie turned her back so she could wipe her eyes.

Birdie tapped her on the back. "Let's dance."

Surrounded by lights from the tree and the reflection of the sun coming through stained glass, they began to twirl.

The director of Hanging Grapes Haven was Evelyn Manchester, an attractive woman in her late forties. From what Lance had seen, she tried hard not to let her heart get involved with the sometimes heartbreaking cases that ended up under her care. Cases such as Birdie's.

He gave Jolie's name as a contact and Evelyn said, "This is great. It's always sad when our residents don't have family."

Homeless was a word he understood all too well. The past tugged at him, and Lance found himself wondering if Birdie had been somebody's mother.

He handed the director his business card. "Put my name down, too."

It was a giant step for a man who never got personally involved. Whether his gesture had to do with the season or Birdie herself, Lance couldn't say. All he knew was that he couldn't walk away from a woman who had no family and no name.

"Now, can you give me her history?"

"Most of what we have is anecdotal. She was brought here by someone from the local Department of Welfare with nothing except the clothes she wore and two books, *Audubon's Field Guide to North American Birds* and *Gone With the Wind*. She's been here nearly twenty years, longer than my tenure.

"Some of the old-timers say she was a hobo who rode in from Chicago on a train. Others say she was an ornithologist before the onset of Alzheimer's. We simply don't know. All we know is that her physical health is good and she's clever enough to escape every now and then."

"She mentioned a person named Jacky," Lance said. "Do you have any idea who that might be?"

"No. She calls several people here by that name. He's real to her, but we have no clue."

Lance thanked her, then went to Birdie's room. He found Jolie dancing with Birdie in a rainbow of Christmas lights and sun catchers. His heart wrenched, and he stood watching from the shadows outside the door for a very long time.

Yes, Virginia, there really is a Santa Claus, he thought, and then he cleared his throat and walked into the room to say goodbye to the Bird Lady.

It was dark when they left the nursing home. Lance took the wheel because Jolie was in no shape to drive. She wasn't the kind of woman who sniffled quietly and dabbed at her hardly mussed face with a delicate handkerchief. No, Jolie bawled with big heaving sobs, her nose turning red and her mascara streaking.

By the time they reached the outskirts of Pontotoc she'd run through a whole pack of tissues. She wadded the wrapper up and tossed it into the stuffed plastic bag hanging from the cigarette lighter.

"I can't quit crying," she wailed.

"That's okay."

She scrambled around in her purse and came up empty-handed. "Elizabeth *always* has a handkerchief."

Holding the wheel with one hand, Lance reached into his pocket, withdrew a handkerchief and handed it to her. "Take mine."

"It'll be a mess."

"That's what washing machines are for."

She blew her nose. "I like you, Lance Estes."

"I like you, too."

Understatement of the year. He was dangerously close to pulling over to the side of the road and taking her into his arms. For comfort, of course, but still....

Gripping the wheel, he watched the darkened scenery. And suddenly there it was…a drive-in theater, the marquee lit with neon, the removable letters listing Jimmy Stewart, his favorite actor, in a double feature: *Harvey* and the Christmas classic *It's A Wonderful Life*

"Would you like to go to the movies?" he asked.

She perked up like a little girl who had been promised ice cream. "What a great idea. I'd love it."

Now he'd done it. Three hours in a car with the

sweetest woman he'd ever met. Lance blamed it on Jimmy Stewart.

Then later, when he reached for her hand, he blamed it on the moon. Halfway through the Christmas feature, when she leaned against his shoulder and he slid his arm around her, it was for comfort, he told himself.

"I'd buy the Brooklyn Bridge from Jimmy Stewart," Jolie said.

And Lance told her, "So would I."

"I'm glad. It says a lot about a man that he can like sentimental movies and a gentle hero."

"What does it say?"

"For one thing, that he has a tender heart."

Lance had never thought of himself as tenderhearted. Occasionally, of course, he did a decent act that others might misconstrue. Still, he liked to think of himself as emotionally uninvolved.

At least, until tonight he'd liked it.

Sighing, Jolie settled closer. "This is nice."

"Yes, it is."

She leaned back so she could see his face. "You don't mind?"

Mind? He was close to taking it up as a full-time occupation. "No, I don't mind."

"Good. I just didn't want you to get the wrong idea."

"Don't worry."

"Okay." She settled back, and he noticed how

perfectly she fit against him. Her head came to just under his chin, and when he rest it in her soft hair he could smell the fragrance she wore, light and sweet as summer flowers.

Lance was aware of every cell in his body, every ounce of blood as it rushed through his veins, the steady thrumming of his heart.

The movie passed in a blur. If his life had depended on repeating what he'd seen on the screen, he couldn't have. For him there was one reality, and that was holding Jolie.

Suddenly her shoulders began to shake.

"Jolie?" He leaned down and caught the sheen of tears in her eyes. "What's wrong?"

"I always cry at the end."

She was soft and appealing, and he was dangerously close to kissing her. He was dangerously close to calling her "precious."

"I'll get popcorn," he said instead. "Do you want it with butter or without?"

"With."

He left her sitting in an appealing little heap on the front seat of a car that had transformed itself into a hotbed of temptation. Striding across the drive-in's parking lot, Lance congratulated himself on his clever escape. With popcorn, they'd both have something else to do with their hands.

But how long would popcorn last? Not through an

entire movie. Especially since they hadn't had anything else to eat since their late lunch.

He bought hot dogs and Cokes, then, fearful of having time on his hands, he added two candy bars. King-size.

"Chocolate," she said when she saw the candy. "Just what I wanted. Are you a mind reader, too?"

"Too?"

"In addition to your many other talents."

Momentarily speechless, he sat there like a dummy wondering what his many talents were. He didn't dare ask.

"Maybe," he finally replied. Instead of looking at her, he dug into his box of popcorn.

"Movie popcorn is always the best," she said. "Don't you think so?"

"Definitely."

"Do you think it's because of the way they pop it, or is it because of the company?"

"The company?"

"Yes. Usually when you go to the movies, you're with somebody you like. I've discovered that doing things with people I like makes the activity more fun."

"I see." Did she consider him fun? Tough, hardworking, cool under pressure—those were the things people usually said about him. But fun? Never.

Much to his relief, she was quiet for a while. Was

it because he'd hurt her feelings? Was it because he didn't make small talk and say *You're fun, too*?

He took a big bite of hot dog but he could hardly taste it for wondering exactly how much Jolie Kat Coltrane liked him. Even more to the point, exactly how much did he like her?

Too much.

The second feature got under way, and they sat on the front seat, separated by a good two feet and enough food to last halfway through the movie.

And then what?

Jolie didn't have a devious bone in her body, but there she was, sitting on her side of the car, trying to think how she could maneuver herself back into Lance's arms. Of course, she hadn't exactly been *in* his arms, but she had been close enough to smell the soap on his skin and enjoy the comfort of his arm across her shoulder.

She ripped into her candy bar and savored the chocolate while Jimmy Stewart conversed with his imaginary rabbit. When In Doubt, Be Bold. That had always been her motto, and although she was in the throes of making herself over, she wasn't planning to ditch philosophy she'd followed her entire life. Just the parts that didn't work.

And so when she finished her candy, she wadded up the wrapper and crammed it into the empty popcorn box, then slid across the seat and leaned into him.

"I hope you don't mind?"

"No."

"Good. You're extraordinarily comfortable."

He didn't say anything. Had she offended him? Did he think she was flirting? Not flirting?

Fighting the urge to fidget, she tried to concentrate on the movie. It was a hopeless task. Finally she risked a peek at him...and fell straight into the depths of his dark eyes.

As he leaned toward her, her breath escaped in a long, drawn-out, "Oohh."

His black hair absorbed the moonlight, then his face blotted it out. His mouth was close, so close. He was going to kiss her.

Excitement surged through her, and she yearned for his lips with an intensity that was as scary as it was unexpected. She wasn't ready for this. She *was* ready for this. It was too soon. It wasn't nearly soon enough. It was madness. It was magic.

"Jolie." His hand cupped her cheek, his lips inched closer.

"Yes?" *Oh, yes, yes, yes.*

"You have chocolate..." his thumb caressed the edge of her mouth "...right there."

Jolie wanted to lick his hand. She wanted to draw his thumb into her mouth. She wanted to laugh. She wanted to cry.

What was the matter with her?

"Hmm," was all she could say.

"Do you always get chocolate on your mouth?" He was still leaning close and she was dangerously near tears.

"Uhm, I guess. I never noticed."

"Well, I did."

Why couldn't she move? Why didn't he?

In a final desperate act of self-preservation, Jolie said, "Thanks," then scooted none too gracefully away under the pretext of looking in her purse for lipstick.

She never bothered to paint her lips after she ate. Poodles and weimaraners didn't care whether she wore lipstick or not. Pet owners didn't, either.

She wasn't even the kind of woman who carried a compact. Working without a mirror, she slashed color on her lips, never mind whether she stayed within the lines. Who would notice anyhow?

The only things Lance noticed about her were her silly mistakes—chocolate smears, comic flak gear, cooking disasters.

That wasn't entirely true. He had called her pretty. Well, she wasn't about to build a whole romance out of one word. She was too busy becoming a new woman. A *wise* new woman.

"Are you watching this movie?" she asked.

"Not really."

"It's late and I'm getting sleepy. Do you mind if we go home?"

"Not at all."

He didn't have to act so grateful. A little reluctance on his part would have salved her wounded pride, though what she had to be wounded about was beyond her comprehension. All he'd done was tidy her up a bit.

Lord, he must think she was the biggest mess in Mississippi.

Tomorrow she was going to change his mind. She didn't know how yet, but she'd think of something.

Chapter Eight

When Jolie's alarm went off at seven, she lay in her bed wondering what had possessed her to get up at such a god-awful hour. Then she remembered: today was the day she would start getting organized.

She left a note for Lance in the kitchen, then drove to the local 24-hour discount store.

Elizabeth would be proud. Jolie was starting today with a list. In fact, the list in her hand was so long she could slipcover Texas with it. Maybe after she got organized she could trim it down to something smaller, say the size of a good longhorn heifer.

She bought everything on her list—multicolored sticky notes, daily desk planner, daily purse-size planner, notebooks to fit pockets and purses and desk drawers, pens and pencils, and enough paper clips to make a chain across the county. Loaded with packages and feeling triumphant, Jolie whizzed back home and dialed her apartment. No messages.

She had hoped to hear news regarding her job interview. Was it too soon? Should she make a follow-up call? Was she too anxious? Too laid-back?

"Jolie?"

Lance was in the doorway, smiling, looking much too appealing for her peace of mind. Memories of sitting in the curve of his arm at the drive-in theater colored her cheeks. Was he remembering? Trying to forget?

Or worse, not even giving last night a second thought?

"Oh, hi. Did you get my note?"

"I did." He studied her until she thought she would burst into flames, then abruptly turned his attention to her packages. "It looks like you bought out the store."

"I needed a few things for my office." Now why had she said that? *Nobody* knew about her job search.

"Your office?"

"Well, not yet. The office I'm going to have." She sighed, and the truth came tumbling out. "If I get the job. Unless the SPCA finds out about me."

"That you wear soccer pads for flak gear?"

"That I'm scatterbrained and flighty and…and un-reliable."

"I can't think of anybody I'd rather have on my team than you."

"Really?"

"Yes. You're fearless and loyal and determined. Those are admirable qualities, Jolie, and don't let anybody tell you differently."

All of a sudden she felt fearless and loyal and determined, a woman to be admired, even if he didn't want to kiss her. Which was fine with her. It really was. She needed to stay focused on her plan.

"Thank you. You won't tell Elizabeth, will you? About the job?"

"No."

Thank goodness he didn't ask why he should keep it secret. Jolie didn't want to talk about being the sibling nobody expected to succeed. She wanted to put the past and her old psychologically crippling baggage behind her.

Lance was studying her again, and she came un-done—shortened breath, hammering heart, racing blood. He moved, adjusting his stance, leaning closer, and Jolie's lips parted.

"Did you miss me?" She licked her bottom lip. "I mean…this morning while I was gone, did you find everything you needed to…to…"

"I missed you."

"You did?"

"Yes."

Oh help, she was drowning. His eyes were amazing and she was floundering in their depths without a clue. Shoot, she didn't even want to be rescued. She wanted to wallow in glorious, total immersion.

"Lance."

His name came out in a sigh. Lovely name. She wanted to take one of her new pens and write "Mrs. Lance Estes" two dozen times in one of her recently purchased notepads just for the pure pleasure of seeing how it looked on paper.

He must have read her mind, because he backed off, not literally, but in ways she could see—body language, facial expression, even his eyes. Everything about him changed from warm and inviting to cool and remote.

"Your mother called while I was in the library. I let the machine take it."

"What did she say?"

"She and the rest of the family will be home in three days."

"Three days!"

"It'll be Christmas Eve."

"Good grief, I'll never be ready by then. I haven't even figured out how to thaw the Christmas turkey, let alone bake it."

"Could you use a hand?"

"A hand? Good Lord, what I need is a miracle."

Lance led her to the kitchen, then tied on her apron and his.

"One miracle, coming up."

Lance always relaxed when he cooked. There was something about the precise measuring and mixing and timing that soothed him. Unlike his job, where anything could happen, there were no surprises in the kitchen…until today.

Jolie added an unheard of element to cooking: fun. She listened to loud music, she danced, she hummed. She made messes, then laughed at herself.

She was lively, charming, fun to be with and impossible to ignore. She was addictive.

"I can't believe this," she said, grinning. "Six casseroles ready to freeze, then take out on Christmas Day and bake. Amazing."

"You have to allow time for thawing."

"Wait…wait. Let me write it down." She caught her tongue between her teeth while she was writing, a little girl's gesture so enticing he reached over and tweaked her pigtail.

"You're going to do great, Jolie."

"Thanks to you, miracle man."

"I take no credit. You just needed a little guidance, that was all."

She scribbled some more. "Wait a minute…. Now what did you tell me about the turkey? I want to be sure I don't end up with a half-baked bird."

He went over the instructions again, then added, "Tomorrow we'll make the congealed salads, and the day after, the desserts. That just leaves the turkey, the green salad and heating the rolls for Christmas Day."

"I can do that."

"I'll help."

"No, no. You've done enough already. More than enough." She sank on to a bar stool, suddenly glum. "I shouldn't have dragged you into this."

"I enjoy cooking."

"Yeah, but not on your vacation, for crying out loud." Tearing up, she began a futile search of her pockets. Why did women cry so often? And why did it make a man feel helpless and strong at the same time?

He searched his own pockets and came up empty-handed.

"I'm nothing but a pack of trouble." She began to cry in earnest, and without a handkerchief, what could he do but kiss her?

He cupped her lovely face and bent over her sweet lips with the full intention of offering nothing more than comfort and reassurance. The kiss turned out to be something else entirely, something so unexpectedly satisfying that he forgot all about rescuing her.

Instead she rescued him. She wrapped her arms around his neck and pressed her heart against his, then threw her whole self into the kiss.

He'd never known anything like it. The sensations of giving and taking were so intermingled that he couldn't tell one from the other. Theirs was a complete merger, not merely a joining of lips but a twining of spirits and souls. Of hearts.

No. Lance broke off and stepped back. Jolie tilted her head and stared at him, flushed and expectant.

"Sorry," he said.

A huge silence roared around them, and then she settled back on to the bar stool, slightly flushed.

"That's okay," she said. "No harm done."

Not yet. If they had continued that kiss, he would have done irreparable harm. He had no intention of leading her to believe that he was the kind of man who could be involved in a romance.

And if he read her correctly, Jolie Kat Coltrane was the kind of woman who would settle for no less. Certainly she wouldn't be interested in a brief fling.

Nor would he. Not with her.

Her sister had been too good to him. Her family had opened their doors to him for what was normally a family-only holiday.

But most of all, Jolie was too important. He couldn't take what he wanted, then walk away. And walking away was exactly what he would do. He was a man who could offer a woman nothing except parttime love interspersed with long periods of fear and uncertainty. He could offer nothing except a borrowed name.

"Since we've finished here, I think I'll ride around awhile," he said. He needed fresh air.

"Great. That sounds like a good idea."

Was she anxious for him to leave? Sincere? Hoping he'd ask her to come? For a man who read people all the time, he had a hard time figuring her out, which was exactly why he had to get away. He was losing touch with reality.

"You can come along if you'd like." Did she notice how halfhearted his invitation was? Probably. Jolie was no dummy.

"Thanks, but I have lots of chores I need to do around here."

"See you later, then." Much later. He planned to stay away till he was certain she'd be in bed. He'd had about all the temptation he could stand for one day.

Lance left the kitchen and didn't look back. Suited up, he roared off on his motorcycle with no destination in mind.

Jolie sat on the bar stool listening to the sounds of his motorcycle die away.

"Okay," she said.

She took a deep breath, then another. "Pull yourself together, girl. It was just a kiss."

With her hand over her lips she relived the last few minutes. Amazing! A kiss was *not* a kiss. Some of them were special.

But then he'd *apologized*. Jolie had thought she would die. How awful to feel on top of the world one minute and down in the doldrums the next.

"I just won't think about it."

If she did she would get depressed and go on a crying jag that would leave her nose red and her eyes swollen and her body feeling as if it had been dumped off a ten-speed bike.

She turned the radio down, then called her mother.

"Hi, Mom. How's California?" She crossed her fingers, hoping that Lucy wouldn't notice she was down in the dumps. Jolie didn't want to spoil her mom's last few days with Aunt Dolly. Naturally, her hope was futile. Lucy could sniff out depression more than a thousand miles away.

"Kat? What's wrong?"

The minute her mother asked, Jolie felt a wave of relief, which just went to show how selfish she was. And at Christmas, to boot.

"You know that man Elizabeth invited here for Christmas?"

"Yes, her friend from Italy."

"He's not Italian."

"Oh, I had hoped he was. Ben and I are thinking of going to Italy next spring and I wanted to get a few language pointers. Does he speak Italian?"

"I didn't ask."

"Tell me about him."

"What is there to tell?"

"I don't know, Kat. You're the one who brought him up."

Jolie sighed. What was there to tell? Did one kiss mean anything?

"He's very nice."

"I'm glad. Knowing Elizabeth, I didn't expect anything less."

"I know. She's perfect."

"All my children are perfect."

"Only to you, Mom."

"My prerogative. Now tell me, what's going on?"

Lucy being a romance novelist, her mind ran naturally toward love, but Jolie was having second thoughts about saying anything whatsoever regarding her confused feelings.

Wasn't that exactly what the family would expect of her? Confusion, even in an arena where everybody else knew exactly what they wanted—if you believed all the magazine articles about dating and marriage. There was supposed to be some sort of instant chemical reaction you could feel, like getting zapped in the heart with a lightning bolt. Only love wouldn't kill you.

Or would it?

Jolie had felt sparks, but had Lance? She wasn't about to go blabbing about her feelings until she knew his. She'd only set herself up for another failure in the eyes of her family.

And so instead of telling Lucy about Lance, she

told her about the Bird Lady. Everything, including the large bill Jolie had run up at the boutique.

"You did the right thing, Kat. Now tell me, did you invite her to Christmas dinner?"

"No."

"By all means, do. The O'Banyon-Coltrane table is always big enough for one more."

"Thanks, Mom. Give Ben and Aunt Dolly a hug for me."

"I will. Dolly's thinking of coming back to O'Banyon Manor for the rest of the holidays."

"Great." Jolie mentally added two more people to the Christmas dinner tally, then started dividing casseroles into servings. Six servings per casserole? Eight? Ten? She'd have to ask Lance.

"Is Kitty home yet?" her mother asked.

"No. Aunt Kitty and Josh aren't coming until Christmas Day."

"I had assumed she was taking care of dinner. You'd better call the caterer, Kat. Call Bonnie Lumpkin. She'll do it on short notice."

"I'm taking care of it, Mom."

"You are? Well, that's just…great."

From her mother's mouth to God's ears. "Don't worry about a thing."

After Jolie hung up she wandered through the house, trying to think what she could do. There were no chores, not really. The cleaning service would come tomorrow, and she was on vacation from her job, and since she hadn't heard a thing about the new job, she was at loose ends.

She picked up the phone to call Birdie and invite her to Christmas dinner, then thought, What the heck, I might as well drive over there and do it in person.

She wanted to see how Birdie was doing. Plus Jolie was lonesome. She'd lived the last six years in an apartment in Memphis all by herself with not even a cat to keep her company. And not once had she suffered this all-consuming I'm-so-lonely-I-could-cry syndrome.

Jolie crammed her hair under a baseball cap, grabbed her purse and set out for Hanging Grapes Haven.

Though it had started to rain, her spirits lifted the minute she got into her little blue car. She loved going places. Turning the radio up, she drove with one hand and kept time on the dashboard with the other, all the while singing along at full volume.

She didn't even notice her audience until he turned the siren on. She pulled over and rolled the window down.

''Going to a fire, lady?''

At first she didn't recognize him huddled in the rain with his coat collar turned up, but then she jerked off her cap and said, ''Sam...Sammy Joe Talbert, is that you?''

''Kat?'' The former quarterback of Shady Grove

High leaned in the window. "Kat Coltrane! I'd know that pigtail anywhere. Are you still raisin' hell?"

"Looks like it."

"It sure does. Did you know you were going fifty-five in a forty-mile zone?"

"I was singing."

"Well, hell, when wasn't you goin' around with your head in the clouds and forgettin' everything except havin' fun? I'm supposed to give you a ticket, Kat."

"Ah, Sammy. It's Christmas."

"Hell, you could be put in jail for a smile like that." He grinned. "Listen, Kat, I'm not gonna ticket you tonight, but slow this thing down, you hear me?"

"Will do, Sammy. I may be fun-loving, but I'm no fool. Merry Christmas."

"You, too."

Jolie waved, then drove off, formerly a happy-go-lucky driver not paying attention, now a cautious blue snail.

Chapter Nine

"Play that song again, Jacky."

Lance put the harmonica back to his mouth, then played "Swing Low Sweet Chariot" for the fifth time while the Bird Lady sat beside her Christmas tree with her head cocked to one side and a faraway look in her eyes.

He hadn't meant to come to Hanging Grapes Haven tonight, but he was glad he had. Birdie was thrilled and kept patting him on the arm and calling him Jacky, which was all right with Lance. Even he didn't know who he really was.

Watching her enjoy the simple pleasure of a mouth harp, Lance thought about growing old without a family, without friends, without even a name except a made-up one a stranger had given him. The blues settled over him and wouldn't go away.

But this time it was a soul-deep ache that felt as if it might settle in permanently unless he did something about it. Like what?

Find out who you are.

Birdie began to sing, "Swing low, sweet chariot, coming for to carry me home...."

Like her, he had no family to call home.

Find out who you are.

He played on while her voice lifted, cracked but surprisingly clear: "I looked over Jordan and what did I see? A band of angels comin' after me...."

Sooner or later the angels would gather them all, but who would claim Birdie? Who would claim him?

Find out who you are.

As Lance finished the song, a flesh-and-blood angel appeared in the doorway—Jolie, her long braid hanging wet underneath a baseball cap flattened by rain, her smile lighting up the room.

"Hi, everybody." Sashaying in with the walk Lance found irresistible, she kissed Birdie on the cheek. "How's my favorite Bird Lady?"

"How come you and Jacky didn't ride together?"

Something flickered across Jolie's face that he couldn't read. "Heck, he's scared to ride with me. I'm hell on wheels. Almost got thrown in jail on the way here."

Was she kidding or not? Keeping his voice neutral, Lance asked, "What happened?"

"I was speeding, but I talked Sammy out of giving me a ticket."

Speeding? In the rain?

Hell!

"That doesn't surprise me," he said, still feigning only moderate interest. "You could talk saints out of their haloes."

She beamed at him. Why had he said that? Beaming was bad for his ragged nerves. Even worse for his libido.

"Well…" She turned her back on him. "Birdie, I just popped in to invite you to Christmas dinner at my house."

"Can I wear my red cowboy boots?"

"You can wear anything you like. I'll come by and get you around two. Is that okay?"

"Will Jacky come, too?"

Jolie glanced over her shoulder. "I'll be there," he said.

"Okay, good, that's settled." Jolie gave Birdie a hug. "Gotta run."

"Wait," Lance said, but she was already out the door.

Wait for what? Another kiss?

Definitely not!

Still, his instincts urged him to leave, urged him to hurry.

"Birdie, I have to go, too."

"Just one more song? Please."

After one verse of "Silent Night," he gave Birdie a quick hug, then hurried out to his motorcycle. There was no sign of Jolie.

How many roads were there from Pontotoc to Shady Grove? Would she take the one he was familiar with?

Trusting she would, Lance buckled on his helmet and set out in pursuit. She couldn't have gotten far, but even going faster than he normally would in the rain, he still didn't see her car.

"Hell." With all his instincts kicked into high gear, he took a curve, then increased his speed. There she was, just up ahead. Filled with relief, Lance chastised himself for getting so dangerously close to caring about her.

He'd gone against his better judgment and taken foolish chances, which just proved that his decision to remain unattached was not only sane and sensible but right.

The rain poured in earnest, but Lance didn't stop to dig out his raincoat. He didn't want to lose sight of Jolie again.

The sign for Shady Grove came into view. Almost there. He'd dry off as soon as he got Jolie safely home.

And breathe again.

Then, helpless and terrified, he watched her car

hydroplane, and prayed she could wrest control from the treacherous, watery stretch of road.

Her car straightened, seemed to be settling down, but then resumed its crazy careening.

In the distance, headlights cut through the gloom. Another car was heading straight toward her, set on a collision course.

Lance relived the awful moment he'd watched a burning building bury his partner.

"No!" he screamed. "God, no!"

Jolie's car swerved right and landed nose down in the ditch as the oncoming car passed safely by. In the aftermath of tragedy, the stillness seemed peculiar and absolute. The only sound was Lance's blood rushing in his ears.

Leaving his bike on the shoulder of the road, he stumbled down into the ditch. It was too dark to see through her window; it was raining too hard to know what lay inside the car.

"Jolie!" No response.

Lance jerked the car door open and his heart froze. Slumped over the wheel, she gave no sign of life.

"Oh my God, Jolie…"

He checked her pulse and found a strong, steady beat. *Thank heavens.* "Jolie, can you hear me? Jolie?"

She groaned and raised her head off the steering wheel. "Where am I? What happened?"

"You skidded off the road… Wait, don't move.

Do you hurt anywhere?'' He leaned across her and turned on the interior lights. There was a small gash on her forehead, but nothing else that he could see.

He brushed her hair back from her forehead and was relieved to see that the skin was barely broken. Nothing that would require stitches.

"I'm okay." In the closeness of the car he was vividly aware of her, of her warm breath fanning across his cheek, of the perfume she wore, of the softness of her skin underneath his hand.

All he could think was I almost lost her.

The car that had passed them turned around in a driveway up the road and headed in their direction. Its headlights cast a halo around her head, so that she appeared to be some sort of disheveled Christmas angel.

His Christmas angel. His tomboy in knee pads, his sprite in a pigtail. His love.

Whoa. Where had that come from? He was over-reacting to the accident, that was it. Had to be.

The man from the car hurried toward them. "God, we saw what happened. It like to'ave scared my wife to death. These curvy country roads can be tricky in weather like this." Big and friendly-faced, his glasses streaked with rain and his navy-blue blazer clinging to him in wet patches, he stood at the edge of the road. "Bill Watkins. You folks need any help down there?"

"Yes, we do," Lance told him. "I've got to get her to the hospital. Call 9ll."

"I'm okay. There's nothing but a little scratch," Jolie insisted.

Ignoring her protests, Lance lifted her from the car.

Sitting in the visitors' waiting room of Shady Grove Hospital, Lance played the moment over and over. He'd lifted her from the car and held heaven in his arms. The shock of awareness was so great that for a moment he'd stood in the bright lights from Bill's car, paralyzed. He hadn't wanted to let her go. Ever.

Standing up now to pace, he glanced at the big round electric clock on the wall. It was after ten. How long had the doctor been with her? Thirty minutes? An hour?

It seemed like an eternity.

What if she had internal injuries? Lance had seen it happen. A person could appear perfectly fine, walk away from a wreck talking and acting normal, and then die of internal hemorrhaging before you could get him to the hospital.

That couldn't happen to Jolie. He wouldn't lose her. He *couldn't*.

Lance grabbed a nurse passing by. "Can you tell me Jolie Katherine Coltrane's condition?"

"The doctor's still with her."

"Is she okay?"

"You'll have to wait and talk to the doctor."

Lance wanted to punch the walls. With a terse, "Thank you," he hurried toward the coffee machine before he made a complete fool of himself.

The lukewarm coffee did nothing to relieve his anxiety. He tossed it into a garbage can, then hurried back to the waiting room. If she got through this...*when* she got through this, he was going to be a changed man. He was going to talk to her, tell her—

"Mr. Estes?" The doctor had silver hair and a name tag that read Harold Clayton, M.D.

"Yes. I'm Lance Estes."

"You're her next of kin?"

Oh God, was she dead?

"No, I'm the one who brought her in. Her relatives are all out of town. How is she?"

"She has an abrasion on her forehead, that's all. She might have a slight headache."

Lance was so relieved he had to sit down. "Anything else, Dr. Clayton?"

"I'd watch her, if I were you."

"What should I watch for? Dizziness? Nausea?"

"Flying missiles. Kat's temper is legendary in Shady Grove, and she's mad as hell about running off the road and you dragging her to the hospital in an ambulance."

Lance would face a grizzly now that he knew she

was okay. He hurried to her room and found her exactly as the doctor had said.

"I am so mad I could hit something," she said.

"Hit me." He sat on the edge of her bed, scooped her into his arms and buried his face in her sweet-smelling hair. "Go ahead, hit me. I make a big target."

Her fists pounded his back and then she began to cry. "I'm such a mess."

"No you're not. You're the dearest thing in my life."

"I am?" Her voice was muffled against his shoulder, and her tears were wetting the front of his shirt.

"Yes, you are, and if I weren't a man without a name, who courts danger for a living, I'd let you know exactly how dear you are."

"You would?" She leaned back to look at him, and he kissed her tenderly on her bruised forehead.

"I would." He brushed her hair back from her face. "Jolie, I'm an orphan from Arizona who doesn't even know who his mother is, let alone his father. And I put my life on the line every day for the International Security Force. I have no business making promises to any woman, let alone a woman like you."

"Like me?"

"Yes, like you." He kissed her softly on the lips. "You're special, Jolie, and don't you ever forget it."

"Oh, Lance." She got stars in her eyes. How

could a woman in her condition do that? And how could he resist her?

If he stayed where he was, he wouldn't be able to, and that was a fact. He'd already said too much, and if he stayed he was liable to say more.

"I've got to see about getting you checked out," he murmured. And then he escaped.

Jolie was in a foul mood. Her head hurt, her car had a dented front fender and the towing bill was bound to cost her a week's salary. Then there was the hospital bill…. Even worse, she'd been nothing but trouble to Lance ever since he'd arrived.

Not that he was complaining. She wished he would. She wished he'd say, "I've spent all evening dealing with ambulances and wreckers and perfect strangers, without whose help I would never have managed to get your car and my motorcycle home." Maybe that would make her feel less like a sinner being cared for by a saint.

In addition, he'd built a cozy fire, insisted she get into a warm robe and slippers, and even fetched an afghan in case she got a chill. Sitting in front of the fire in the library at O'Banyon Manor with a lump as big as a hen's egg on her forehead, she felt like a complete fool. She had run off a road that was as familiar to her as the back of her hand.

Furthermore, she hadn't even been speeding. She knew better, especially after that warning from Sam.

How did she manage to do the wrong thing even when she was trying to do right? That's what she wanted to know.

And in front of Lance, of all people.

"Do you want more hot chocolate?" he asked.

"No, thank you."

"Another pillow?"

"I'm fine, thanks."

"Are you warm enough?" He got up and poked the fire. "I can add another log."

"The fire's just right."

"Or get another blanket. Do you need another blanket?"

"For Pete's sake!" she snapped. "Stop hovering."

If she hadn't been so miffed she'd have laughed at the little-boy-caught-with-his-hand-in-the-cookie-jar look on his face.

"I don't hover."

"Yes, you do. Just stop it. I can take care of myself."

"Not from where I'm sitting."

She let that pass. After all, he had rescued her from the ditch, and if it hadn't been for him there was no telling what would have happened. On the other hand, if it hadn't been for him, she might have had her mind on the road.

What had happened to the intimacy at the hospital? Well, not *intimacy,* not really, but he had been holding her and giving her tender kisses and telling her about himself. It had been so wonderful that she'd hoped it would last forever.

Jolie stared into the fire and tried to center herself. She tried to think positive, reassuring thoughts, but her mind was a cage with a wild squirrel let loose inside.

In two days her family would be home. She had a knot on her head they'd all notice, plus she was about two thousand light years away from having dinner prepared. She made a royal mess of everything, including her not-quite relationship with Lance.

"Don't you think you ought to be in bed?" he said.

"Oh *Lord*." She threw off the afghan, then marched to the fire and picked up the poker. "Why don't you go somewhere?"

"I'm not leaving you alone."

"I didn't mean leave the house, I just meant *do something*."

His eyes took on the predatory gleam of a panther as he headed her way. "All right."

She didn't like this. Not one bit.

He was so close she could see the beard shadow on his jutted-out, hell-bent-for-leather jaw.

"What are you doing?"

"I'm going to kiss you."

Oh, help.

"Why?"

"To keep you from biting my head off." He caught her shoulders and she melted all the way down to her toes. "And because I'm so damned relieved that you're alive."

The kiss curled her toes, shot off rockets in her head, made comets blaze through her mind. If she'd thought his other kisses had been special, she hadn't known what special was. This one was off-the-scale wonderful. It was amazing, mind-boggling, magical.

She couldn't get close enough. She wanted to absorb every inch of him, merge with his magnificent chest, then vanish inside his steadily beating heart.

He deepened the kiss and she felt how his body responded to her, how hers responded to him.

She wove her hands in his hair and pulled him closer, and he deepened the kiss. If they kept this up her knees would buckle, but the rug was plush and she was ready. More than ready. She was on fire.

"Jolie," he murmured against her lips.

And she whispered back, "Yes, oh yes."

He inched away, then gazed into her eyes for a small eternity, and she saw passion as plain as if it had been written on his face with an ink pen.

Never had she wanted anything as much as she wanted him, right then, right there. She knew the exact moment he changed his mind. A giant eraser—probably called *conscience*—swooped down and wiped his face clean.

He stepped back, and he didn't have to say anything. In fact, she didn't want him to speak. She would save them both the humiliation.

"I'm going to bed," she said.

She stalked upstairs, pulled the covers up to her chin and told herself she was not going to think about Lance Estes.

Except maybe a teensy bit.

Chapter Ten

As he watched her stalk off, Lance called himself fifty kinds of a fool. He was playing with fire. Worse, he couldn't seem to help himself. His attraction for her was the dangerous kind, the kind that tugged at his heart.

His problem was how to keep the attraction from becoming fatal. A man without a name had no business falling in love with a woman like Jolie, a woman who deserved everything.

But what if he had a name to offer her? The mission of finding his roots took on a sudden urgency.

Setting up his laptop on the mahogany desk, he tapped into the vast resources of the ISF and began a search for his first housemother at the orphanage.

It didn't take him long to locate her. Ina Estes, now married to Lawrence Clancy, lived in Phoenix, Arizona. Lance called information, and in another stroke of good luck, found her phone number listed. Even with the time difference it was too late to call and say, "I'm Lancelot from Sunshine Acres Orphanage, and I'm searching for my birth mother."

He would make that call in the morning. He didn't want to know why he'd been abandoned or whether he had been loved. He merely wanted to know his name.

Jolie woke up with only a slight headache. She took an aspirin and inspected the lump on her head. It had turned a garish purple with a sickly yellow perimeter. Her mother would see it and imagine death by internal bleeding. Her siblings would see it and think, That's Kat for you. Same old klutz. Aunt Kitty would get out the herbal remedies and Aunt Dolly would either ignore it or make a big joke of it, both with high drama.

Jolie tried to cover the bruise, but makeup only called attention to it, and in addition made her look like somebody trying out for the circus. There was only one thing to do.

She pulled on jeans and a T-shirt, then scavenged in the medicine cabinet until she found a pair of scissors. Unfortunately, they were the kind used to cut bandages, but they'd have to do.

She picked up a hunk of hair, held her breath and cut. The scissors were dull, but Jolie remained undaunted. Taking a fortifying breath, she made another brave cut. Then another.

The pile of hair in the sink grew, but she had plenty left, so she was determined not to be alarmed. Bangs would hide the bruise. Anybody could cut bangs.

She made her final cut, then stood back to inspect her handiwork. The bangs were a bit uneven and more than a little ragged, but underneath a cap, who would know?

Of course, she couldn't wear a baseball cap all the time or her family would get suspicious. *Hair gel.* Now there was the solution.

Jolie worked with her bangs, hoping for a creative, mod look. What she got was sticky hands and a hidden bruise.

"Oh well."

She had other things to worry about. Christmas dinner, for one. Making it without Lance's help, for another.

It was time for her to stand on her own two feet. If she ever wanted to become a new woman, she'd better quit depending on him and start doing things for herself.

Thank goodness he was nowhere around. For one thing, she wanted to get the baking underway, by herself. Also, she wasn't ready to face him after last night's kiss.

She donned her apron, grabbed her cookbook and laid out her mixing bowls. Usually she plunged in right away, but this time she read the entire recipe step by step before she did anything. Lance had taught her that.

That wasn't all he'd taught her.... Memories of last night's kiss threatened to undo her.

She turned the radio up to drown out her distracting thoughts, and had just started mixing the cake when the phone rang.

It was Aunt Kitty.

"Jolie, I have great news. Do you remember Josh's friend Michael Sullivan?"

She remembered having a mad crush on him. He was blond and fun to be with, a wild Irish version of Brad Pitt. But then she'd been only sixteen the last time she saw him, and prone to flights of fantasy.

"The one who dropped out of seminary to become a private eye?"

"An undercover cop with Chicago PD," Aunt Kitty corrected her. "Anyhow, he's coming to Christmas dinner."

"Great," she said. But another guest, another casserole, was what she was thinking.

"I know. Josh is so excited. It has been years since he saw Michael."

"I'm glad he can join us." Jolie mentally tried to

stretch the turkey for…what was the count up to now? Fifteen people?

"We're bringing a honey-baked ham." Jolie's sigh of relief was cut short by Aunt Kitty's next statement. "We decided to come tomorrow instead of waiting. There's always so much traffic on the road Christmas Eve."

"Wonderful," Jolie said. What she was thinking was Help!

After she hung up, she set about baking with a vengeance.

Okay, I can do this. I can do this.

Aunt Kitty had just lopped a whole day off her cooking time. But what was one day? Jolie would simply work into the night.

Lance heard the music coming from the kitchen before he smelled the sweet, spicy fragrance of baking. He pictured Jolie humming and moving to the lively music, and his hormones immediately went into overdrive.

He started to bypass the kitchen altogether and head straight to the gym in the basement.

Coward.

The music was loud and she was dancing, just as he imagined. Unnoticed, he catalogued every detail: her long ponytail swaying to the beat of B. B. King, the tufted, punk-rock bangs, the crooked chocolate cake with the split-apart top.

"Oh!" She put her hand over heart. "I didn't hear you come in."

"Good morning." Trying to act normal, he headed to the coffeepot. "New hairdo?"

"Yes. Does it cover the bruise?"

"It does." He could guess why she'd done it: the bruise was another badge of failure. Touched, he added, "The bangs look nice."

"You really think so?"

"Yes. They're sassy and lively. Like you." He poured two cups of coffee and hoped she'd wouldn't notice how deeply personal his observation was.

She was wearing perfume again, the fragrance that clouded his senses and settled over him like a caress. He sat on a bar stool as far away from her as possible.

"I see you started the baking without me."

"Yes. Actually, I want to do it all by myself. I *need* to." She picked up the platter holding the pitiful, lopsided chocolate cake. "What do you think?"

"Congratulations. You did it."

"Yeah, except the top layer split."

"A little extra icing will fix that."

She caught her tongue between her teeth, and he nearly came undone. Gripping his coffee cup, he tried to ignore that sweet, pink tongue.

"Listen, Lance… I'm sorry about last night…that I was so much trouble and all."

"No problem."

He stared at her, every nerve jingling, alive in ways he'd never believed possible. The telephone jarred him out of his spell.

When Jolie answered, he picked up his coffee and started to leave, but she motioned for him to stay put. With her hand over the mouthpiece, she said, "It's just Elizabeth."

Sipping his coffee, he watched Jolie's expression change from lively good humor to growing alarm.

"Well," she said to her sister, "isn't that great?... No, no, it's wonderful...the sooner the better."

"What's wrong?" Lance asked after she'd hung up.

"Elizabeth is not coming home the day after to-morrow."

"What happened? Did her flight get cancelled?"

"No." Jolie plopped on to the bar stool beside him, the picture of defeat. "She got through filming early and changed her ticket. She's coming home *to-night.*"

He clung to his coffee cup, staunchly resisting the urge to put his arms around her and say, "There, there, sweetheart."

"I'll never get all this done with her breathing down my neck," Jolie said, then told him about the rest of the family and the guests they were bringing along.

"Yes, you will." Lance set down his coffee, picked up the spatula and began to patch the split cake with icing. "We'll finish today. I'm going to help you."

"I don't know. Maybe I should just call the deli."

"Is that what you want to do?"

"No. If I have Christmas dinner catered after saying I was going to cook it, I'm living up to everybody's expectations."

"All right, then. Roll up your sleeves and let's get to work. We'll have everything except the turkey done by the time Elizabeth's plane arrives."

"But still, I won't be the one who did it."

"Yes, you will. I'm merely going to pitch in and help."

"I don't know."

"I do." He tied on his apron. "This is an emergency. Get your cute little butt moving."

This turn of events gave him the perfect excuse to be near Jolie all day. If the untimely descent of relatives hadn't occurred, what excuse would he have found? Watching her sweet face and the quick movements of her small hands, noticing how she never got near the flour canister without coming away smudged, hearing how she hummed under her breath even when she didn't know the tune, Lance knew he would have moved heaven and earth to spend this last day alone with her.

Even if he was determined to keep his hands off of her, even if she didn't know how he softened every time she looked up and smiled at him, he was still grateful for this gift of time with the woman who had somehow found her way through his barriers and into his heart.

Cakes and pies and cookies were lined up in a row on the cabinets, all neatly covered with plastic wrap. Congealed salads and casseroles waiting to be baked crowded the shelves of the refrigerator. Ingredients for a green salad were sliced and bagged separately, waiting to be assembled.

The dishes were clean, the kitchen spotless.

What Jolie wanted was to collapse into a hot tub and not move for two hours. What she had was barely enough time to get to the airport to meet Elizabeth's plane.

"I'll go pick her up," Lance said.

"No. I will." She amended her statement because of manners. "Thank you, anyhow."

"It's still raining."

"I *know* that. I can drive in the rain."

He gave her that look. Lord, if she didn't want so badly to hug him, she'd strangle him.

"Be careful," he finally said.

"Don't worry."

She left him standing in the kitchen doing just that. She could tell by the way he stood, stiff-backed and tight-faced. Why did she always manage to have that affect on him?

Maybe she was fated to be the kind of woman who

worried a man to death, instead of a well-put-together, take-charge woman like Elizabeth, who could melt a man's heart with a single glance. That is, if Elizabeth wanted to. Her sister was not the romantic kind. Unlike Jolie, who had thought of nothing except romance ever since Lance came to Shady Grove.

She headed to the airport, wondering whether Lance might have kissed her tonight if they'd been alone, and whether Elizabeth would notice the dent in Jolie's car.

Lance stood in the kitchen listening to the silence and dealing with his inner tumult. Elizabeth's early homecoming changed everything. There would be no more cozy fireside evenings for two. No more chances to give in to temptation. Why didn't he feel relieved?

Rather than dwell on Jolie, he seized the opportunity to make his call to Arizona.

Ina answered on the first ring.

"I don't know whether you'll remember me, but this is Lancelot from Sunshine Acres."

"Oh, my goodness! Of course I do. How wonderful to hear from you."

Now that his private investigation was actually under way, he felt a certain reluctance. Fear of what he would discover? Fear of change? He didn't know.

"Merry Christmas," he said.

"The same to you. Tell me, do you have a family now?"

"No, but I'm hoping you can help me. I'd like to try to locate my mother."

There was a long pause, and then Ina said, "I was wondering when you'd ask."

"Then you know her?"

"Not exactly, but I've always had my suspicions. There was a lovely young girl named Sarah who used to drop by the orphanage selling cookies she and her mother made."

Lance's intuition kicked into high gear. The information *felt* right.

"I know it's not much to go on, but she was always interested in the children, particularly you. I would watch her watching you, and wonder. There were times when I wanted to ask her, but I never did. We had a policy that if a child was left with us, healthy, we didn't interfere. She was so young. No more than fifteen, I'd say."

"Do you know the rest of her name or where she is now?"

"No, but I think I can find out."

After he had hung up, Lance couldn't sit still. Taking his harmonica from his pocket, he went into the garden where one red rose was still blooming, and started to play "Swing Low Sweet Chariot."

Chapter Eleven

"Lancelot!" Elizabeth, who didn't have a hair out of place after being on a plane for hours, launched herself into Lance's arms for a hug that stung Jolie all the way to her toes.

Or maybe she was still stung because Elizabeth had not only noticed the dented fender, she'd ferreted out the cause.

Jolie was turning into a regular Grinch. A jealous Grinch. Why hadn't she known Lance's name was Lancelot? Why hadn't he told her? Why hadn't she asked?

It fit, of course. All that knight in shining armor business about taking care of damsels in distress. And Lord knew, *distress* was her middle name.

Elizabeth hugged him for two hours—that's what it felt like to Jolie's green-monster mind—then got big-eyed over the cookies and coffee he'd set out on a silver tray.

"Look at this." Elizabeth nibbled on a chocolate chip cookie while Jolie recalled every last detail of how it had been made: her gobbling up raw cookie dough, while Lance laughingly threatened her with a spoon.

Elizabeth would never gobble. She wouldn't touch raw cookie dough with a ten-foot pole.

"I thought you might be hungry after your long flight," he told Elizabeth.

"How sweet of you." She patted his cheek. Shoot, Jolie didn't even have the courage to hug him after all his help today. Why couldn't she at least have patted his cheek? "These are delicious. Homemade?"

"Yes," he said, and Jolie was about to tell her sister that Lance had made them when he said, "Jolie made them."

"You did?"

"Well, actually…"

"She cooked all day," Lance said. "You ought to see what else she has in the kitchen."

That took the wind right out of Elizabeth's sails. "I'm beat from the flight. I hope you two don't mind if I crash?"

"Not at all." Jolie sounded like somebody eager

to get rid of her sister. Which wasn't the case. Not really. She gave Elizabeth a heartfelt hug. "Rest up. I want to hear all about your film tomorrow."

"I'll help with your bags," Lance offered.

Elizabeth smiled at him. "Always the gallant one."

The two of them left with big smiles on their faces, and that was that.

Jolie wasn't about to wait around in the library like a spider after a fly. She had more important things to do.

Heck, the entire fate of Christmas dinner hinged on whether her toenails were painted red or something more festive—say, purple with gold glitter.

She holed up in her room and spent an hour with cotton balls, polish remover, cuticle cream, buffing boards and six colors of polish, telling herself that she was busy.

Then the door next to hers opened and closed. *Lance.* Her breathing quickened as she heard the French doors to their shared balcony open.

Jolie debated the question, should she or shouldn't she?

What the heck. It was her balcony, too.

Lance had been leaning against the balcony railing looking at the moon when Jolie walked through the French doors. Backlit by lamps from her bedroom and polished by a silvery winter moon, she took his breath away.

"I heard you out here."

He loved that about her: no artifice.

"I'm unwinding." The truth. Partially. *Thinking of you was the rest of the story.*

She padded across the tiles and leaned against the wrought-iron railing. Barefoot. Toenails shooting sparks in the moonlight. *Lord, everything about this woman was appealing. Even her feet.*

"Thank you for giving me credit in front of Elizabeth for making the cookies. You didn't have to do that."

"I wanted to."

Jolie tipped her face up to the moon while he stood there riveted, listening to the rush of his own blood.

"It's beautiful," she said, looking back at him.

"Yes. Very beautiful."

She sucked in a surprised little breath, then stood there frozen, her pink tongue slowly licking her full bottom lip.

"How's your head?" he asked.

"Oh." She put her hand on her forehead, then winced. "Fine."

"Let me see." Closing the space between them, he brushed her hair back from her face. *Mistake.* The passion between them was palpable, irresistible.

He folded her close, his mouth descended on hers, and time and place slipped away. It wasn't a nameless orphan invading the home and the lips of a woman whose pedigree probably went all the way back to seventeenth-century nobility. There was only a man kissing a woman, a man with his common sense on hold and a woman with the sweetest lips this side of heaven.

The sweetest lips, the sweetest body. Molded against her, Lance felt branded. He knew he should back off, knew he should refrain from goading the beast that rode him hard, but urgency was not easy to ignore. His desire demanded relief, and so he deepened the kiss, hauled her hips closer.

The kittenish, wanting sounds she made inflamed him, and he delved his tongue inside her mouth for a heady exploration that made her sag against him.

It would be so easy to take her. If he didn't stop soon, it would be *necessary.*

Still, Lance couldn't let her go. He couldn't lose this fleeting paradise.

Why was that? He was no monk. He'd had his share of flings, his taste of some of the world's most beautiful women.

How could a mere wisp of a girl, a lively sprite partial to baseball caps, loud music and soccer pads, have embedded herself so deeply under his skin that he couldn't get her out? How could she bewitch him to the point that he acted irrationally, irresponsibly and totally out of character?

His bedroom was just through the French doors.

He longed to carry her inside and possess her. He longed to lose himself in her and forget that he was a no-name orphan in a dangerous career.

Fitted perfectly against him, Jolie was on the edge of surrender. He was on the edge of losing control.

The moon softened his willpower; the delicious sounds she made threatened to sabotage it. With superhuman effort, Lance grabbed the fringes of sanity and wrested himself back under control.

Jolie would have toppled if he hadn't held on to her. His breathing came in harsh bursts as he backed off a fraction, still holding her upright.

He opened his mouth to say *I'm sorry,* but that would be a lie. His only regret was that he had no right to the paradise she offered.

Furthermore, something in her eyes warned him that *sorry* was not the word she wanted to hear.

"Your feet are going to get cold out here," he finally said.

"My *feet?*"

He nodded, and she stood there silently, her cheeks still flushed with passion.

Electric with desire, he held on to her as long as he dared. When he thought he could walk without pain, he said, "Good night, Jolie."

Inside the privacy of his bathroom, he stripped, then climbed into the shower, his face turned up to the icy blast of water. He would not allow what had almost happened tonight to happen again.

Not until he had something to offer her.

* * *

Stunned, Jolie stood on the patio with her arms wrapped around herself and her feet getting cold. It would serve him right if she froze to death. It would serve him right if the temperature dropped twenty degrees and it started sleeting and her whole body turned into an icicle.

As if she wasn't having a hard enough time reining in her galloping libido, her head started to hurt.

The pain made her forget revenge. She stomped inside, but didn't get nearly the effect she'd hoped for. Bare feet made muffled sounds.

Inside her bedroom she stuffed her cold feet into a pair of warm, fuzzy sleep socks, and then, because she couldn't seem to stop shivering, she put on a flannel nightgown, nevermind that the temperature inside the house was a comfortable seventy.

It would serve Lance right if she got so hot in the middle of the night she melted. And she just might. That's the way she felt around him.

Was she falling in love?

She climbed into her bed and pulled up the covers. She didn't have time for life's larger questions. She had to get a good night's sleep. Tomorrow Aunt Kitty, Josh and Michael would arrive; then the day after, her brother and his family, her mother, Ben, Aunt Dolly and no telling who else.

And Jolie had to feed them all.

* * *

Jolie usually popped out of bed first thing in the morning, raring to go. But on the very morning she wanted to be the first one downstairs, she overslept. She glared at the offending clock—it was already ten!—then raced into the bathroom and stood horrified in front of the mirror. The bangs she'd cut, then slicked with gel, the day before now stood up like porcupine quills. In addition to being late from oversleeping, she would have to shampoo her hair, which would make her the last person downstairs.

And that meant she'd miss everything—what Elizabeth said to Lance, what he said to her.

Disgruntled, Jolie climbed into the shower and lathered her hair. Not that it mattered what Elizabeth said to Lance. Her sister would never be disloyal to Jolie, but still…Elizabeth had the irritating habit of portraying her as somebody who shouldn't be let out of the house without supervision.

Jolie made quick work of her hair, then hopped out of the shower and grabbed the blow dryer. Her bangs didn't look half bad now that the rest of her hair was out of the braid. Everything blended in.

Lance had said her bangs suited her. Maybe he was right.

But then, he had a habit of always saying things that made her feel good. Was that why she liked him so much? Was that why she couldn't wait to get him alone in the dark? Was that why she was falling in love?

Oh, help.

With her hair dryer poised in midair, Jolie relived last night's kiss on the balcony. If he hadn't backed off she'd surely have ended up in his bed. And what would be wrong with that?

Couldn't she become a new woman while she was falling in love?

Encouraged by that thought, she grabbed her jeans, then changed her mind and put on black boots, a long black skirt and a soft red cashmere sweater. There was no need to lie about why, either. She was doing it so Lance would notice her.

When she was in a room with her older sister, people usually carried on over Elizabeth until they remembered their manners and said, "And Jolie, you look nice, too."

She sighed. Oh, Lord, she was turning into an awful, jealous person that nobody could love. Not even a mother.

She gave her bangs one last fluff, then headed downstairs to join Elizabeth and Lance. Laughter drifted up the stairs. And voices, one of which she didn't recognize.

Leaning over the banister, she saw her cousin Josh, her aunt Kitty and a man who could only be Michael Sullivan: if the blond hair wasn't enough, the Irish brogue was a dead giveaway.

"So...Lizzie." He grabbed Elizabeth's hands. "We meet again."

Michael Sullivan was the only man in the world who had ever called her sister "Lizzie" with impunity. She hated nicknames, particularly that one. She said it made her sound like somebody's cow.

But there she was, standing in the downstairs hallway, smiling as if he had just crowned her queen of England, and allowing him to hang on to her hands, to boot. No, not just allowing it. Loving it. You couldn't mistake her glow for anything but pure pleasure.

"How long has it been?" Elizabeth asked. "Nine years?"

"Ten. I've been counting the days."

"You're full of Irish blarney."

"And you're as full of beauty as that wee red rose I saw blooming outside your door."

Her sister was flirting.

Jolie hurried down the stairs and received another shock. Elizabeth was actually blushing.

Michael saw her on the stairs. "Look who just arrived. Is that you, Kat?"

"It's me."

He bounded over, swept her in the air and spun her around. "Look at you, still cute as a button."

Lance watched them with a face closed tight as a bank vault. Elizabeth was watching, too, smiling in a way that would fool a perfect stranger. But it didn't fool Jolie. Her sister was faking it.

Good grief. Will wonders never cease? Elizabeth, feeling threatened by me!

Here was Jolie's golden opportunity to indulge in a little game: pit Michael against Lance and put her sister in a bad light by goading her.

But Jolie abhorred games. And she loved her family fiercely.

So what if everything came easily for Elizabeth, even striking sparks with a man she hadn't seen in ten years? If Elizabeth wanted Michael Sullivan, then Jolie was determined to see that she got him.

When Michael put her down, Jolie hugged her aunt Kitty and Josh, then announced, "Would anybody like a cookie? I'm starving to death."

"So am I," Lance said. "Ravenous." The way he looked at Jolie made her feel hot all over. "Why don't I help you serve them?"

He caught her hand, then whisked her off before anybody could say anything. She felt five-eleven and stunning. She felt glamorous and sexy.

And she felt limp all the way to her toes. Melted.

Alone with the copper-bottomed pots and the sweets lined in a row, Jolie and Lance stared at each other, vividly aware, hands still linked.

"I'm beginning to love kitchens," he said.

"So am I."

You could have lit bonfires from her skin. You

could have baked a whole Christmas turkey. With the stuffing. And two pumpkin pies.

"You're beautiful," he said.

"Thank you. I thought the red sweater would be festive."

"The sweater's beautiful, too."

Her head grew too big for her baseball caps. Her heart nearly beat right out of her chest.

Was he going to kiss her? She could almost feel it, taste it. She licked the imaginary sweetness off her bottom lip.

"Don't do that," he said.

"What?"

"That sexy thing with your tongue."

Excited almost beyond control, and nervous, too—what if somebody caught them in the kitchen kissing?—she did it again.

"It makes me want to kiss you."

Jolie had never known a man like him—intense, tightly wired, his voice husky with passion, his eyes sparking fire.

"Then do," she said.

She might as well have poured cold water on him. He left her standing there with her heart on her sleeve and her lips unkisssed.

His back stiff with resolve, he started sorting cookies on to a platter. Without pausing to reconsider, Jolie went over to the cabinet and put her hand on his back.

"Lance, what's wrong?"

She didn't know where this new boldness came from. Maybe it was the red sweater. Maybe it was her sister's example.

"I can't be who you need, Jolie."

"How do you know what I need?"

What a foolish question. He knew everything she needed, because he'd been taking care of her since he got there.

Naturally, he couldn't be who she needed. It would take the whole United States Army to take care of a mess like Jolie Kat Coltrane.

When he didn't answer her, she stomped to the refrigerator without muffling her anger, and let the cold air hit her flaming face.

"Do you think they'll want cold drinks or coffee?"

Her voice trembled only a little. She was turning into an actress. She was turning into her mother.

"Both," he said.

"Okay."

It was the cold drinks that gave her away. One of the traitorous bottles jumped out of her hand and committed suicide against the kitchen tiles.

I will not cry. I will not cry...much.

Lance reached into his pocket and handed her his handkerchief, then put his hand on her shoulder.

"How silly of me," she said, trying to be brave and failing miserably.

Lance pulled her into his arms and rubbed her back. With his face buried in her hair, he said, "I can't abuse your family's hospitality by playing around with the youngest offspring."

Rage dried up her tears. Jerking away, she said, "Don't I get a say?"

For a heart-stopping instant she thought he was going to take her into his arms and kiss her.

"No." His voice was dark and dangerous. "Trust me, Jolie. And stop looking at me with those starry eyes. If I kiss you again I won't be able to stop." He grabbed a cloth and started cleaning up her mess.

Again.

She wanted to hit something. Preferably him.

Chapter Twelve

Lance was acutely aware of Jolie watching him. It took superhuman effort not to take her into his arms and kiss her. He longed to smooth back her sassy bangs, kiss the bruise on her forehead and say, "I'm falling in love with you, but now is neither the time nor the place."

But he wouldn't do that, because he didn't know whether there would ever be a right time for them.

He might never be able to give Jolie a name. He might die on the job the next time out. Or the time after that.

No, best to pretend indifference while she picked up the cookies and walked away.

He wiped the cloth viciously across the floor. How quickly he had forgotten his resolution to avoid all repeat performances of last night's balcony scene. She made it so easy to forget. She almost made it easy to love.

He had too many issues and no business thinking that way. The best thing for him to do would be to leave as soon as possible.

But he couldn't leave before Christmas dinner. That was Jolie's big cooking debut, and he wanted to see her succeed. He owed her that much.

He flung the debris into the garbage can, washed his hands and then braced himself to face her. He should be able to pull it off, especially with other people in the house. He and Elizabeth had a lot of catching up to do, and he'd instinctively liked their cousin Josh.

That Sullivan character was another matter. A man that smooth and easy with women would bear watching.

And that's what Lance intended to do.

The family and their too-exuberant guest were gathered around the cookies, oohing and aahing, which meant Jolie was the center of attention. Lance was as pleased as if he were Professor Higgins watching his protégée.

''Kat made these,'' Elizabeth said.

And then that Irish Romeo popped up and said, ''Best cookies I ever ate.''

Lance planned to be on that guy's case like white on rice. If Michael Sullivan thought he was going to get by with anything in this family, he'd be in for a big surprise.

It was the longest day of Jolie's life. For starters, Lance completely ignored her. To make matters worse, the garrulous Michael Sullivan had to have a blow-by-blow account of what Elizabeth had been doing for the past ten years. Her history sounded like a profile out of America's Outstanding Women. Then, naturally, he had to know what Jolie had been up to. She summarized her career in five words: "I'm a beautician for animals."

Josh rescued her. "Hey, let's have a jam session."

"Grab your blues harp, Lance," Elizabeth said. Although she looked like an unapproachable princess most of the time, she really let her hair down at the piano. She sounded like Jerry Lee Lewis in his hey-day.

Michael Sullivan fetched his guitar and joined in, then—wouldn't you know it?—said to her, "Hey, Kat, what do you play?"

"I keep time with my foot," she said, and he laughed as if she rivaled the stand-up comics on *Saturday Night Live.*

By the time the day was finally over, Jolie couldn't relax. She tangled herself in the covers fifty different ways before she gave up and decided to go down to the kitchen for a big glass of milk and some cookies. Comfort food.

It was after midnight, so she tiptoed, hoping not to wake anybody. She was still tiptoeing when she eased open the kitchen door…and there was Michael Sullivan, barefoot and shirtless in tight jeans that ought to be declared illegal on a man with a body like his. And Elizabeth, in pajamas she'd probably bought in Italy at one of those upscale boutiques catering to women who wished to drive men mad, but in an elegant way.

They didn't see her. How could they? They were locked together in a steamy embrace that would have been given a triple X rating at the movies.

Trying not to breathe, Jolie eased backward. But her luck was bad. Michael saw her and discreetly stepped away. Elizabeth kept her composure, and even managed to look dignified while holding her top together.

"I got the munchies," Jolie said.

"So did we," Michael said. "These are really good cookies, Kat. And you made them, huh?"

"Well, yeah, uh, listen, I'll just grab a glass of milk and head on back." Why should her sister deprive her of a midnight snack? Jolie went to the refrigerator and was extra careful not to drop the milk.

"Nonsense," Elizabeth said. "I was just leaving."

Her exit made royalty look sloppy. Jolie would have felt bad about interrupting what was obviously a hot love scene if she hadn't seen the silent signal that passed between Michael and her sister.

Well, didn't that just make her day? Not that Jolie was jealous, but *everything* came easily for Elizabeth. Just once wouldn't you think something would come easily for Jolie?

She was going to get her snack and vanish into her jungle of bedcovers, but Michael straddled a bar stool, acting as if he planned to stay there all night.

"You know, I've always liked your family, Kat."

"I'm calling myself Jolie now."

"Any particular reason?"

"Yeah, I'm making a few changes in my life."

"Me, too. I'm leaving undercover and taking a desk job with the Chicago PD. It makes more sense for a man planning to settle down and raise a big family."

Since when? Since he'd met Elizabeth?

"That's nice." Jolie forgave herself the lame response. After all, if you've just been caught spying— though it was all perfectly innocent—you couldn't be expected to be witty.

"I come from a big family, you know," he said. "They're all in Boston. I decided to do something different for Christmas this year." He grinned at her. "Boy, am I glad I did."

"I would guess so."

Michael Sullivan threw back his head and laughed.

"I really like you, Jolie. You've got your feet firmly planted and your head out of the clouds."

That's when Lancelot Estes walked in. Naturally. He took one look at her in an oversize nightshirt with a big slogan on the front that said Woman with an Attitude, Don't Stand between Me and My Chocolate. Then he glared at Michael Sullivan with his abundant chest hair and his broad grin. Lance was putting two and two together and getting midnight rendezvous in the kitchen.

How long had he been standing there? Even if he'd overheard the entire conversation between her and Michael, he would still think they were up to hanky-panky.

Lord, that's all she needed: the man she practically swooned over thinking she went up in flames with him on the balcony one night, then messed around with somebody else over baked sweets the next.

"I just came down for a snack," Lance said. You could strike matches on his face. "Obviously, somebody else had the same idea."

Jolie held up her glass of milk. To prove her innocence? Because she was speechless with unrequited passion?

Michael Sullivan never lost his cool. "You bet," he said. "Jolie makes the best cookies in three states." He grabbed a handful to show he meant what he said, then left her to face the music.

Or in this case, the warrior with battle on his mind.

"Sorry I interrupted," Lance said.

"You didn't interrupt anything."

"With your family in the house, you'd think he'd have the decency to put on his clothes."

"Look, we were just—"

"You don't owe me any explanations."

Misjudged and beleaguered from all sides, Jolie couldn't endure the world's longest day anymore.

"I certainly don't." She jerked up her glass of milk and marched toward the door.

"Jolie."

"Go drive somebody else crazy. I'm going to bed."

She stormed out and didn't look back. By the time she got to her room she wasn't even hungry. And she was too mad to sleep. She'd probably never sleep again.

Lance stood in the kitchen wondering just whose bed she was going to.

Terminally charming men like Michael Sullivan shouldn't be turned loose on the world's unsuspecting innocents. Jolie wouldn't know a ladies' man if one fell out of an apple tree and hit her on the head. She wouldn't know a con man if he wore a tattoo declaring his devious intent.

Lance jerked a glass out of the cabinet and poured milk. What business was it of his? He had no claims on her. Other than a sweet little old lady in a nursing home, they had nothing in common.

If you didn't count passion with the punch of a rocket.

"Forget it."

Now she had him talking to himself. That, in addition to acting like a jackass over Michael Sullivan.

Next thing you knew he'd be calling the man out for a duel under a live oak tree.

God, he was losing it. And Lance had one more day to get through before Christmas dinner. Plus another night.

Tomorrow he'd go over to Pontotoc and visit Birdie. One hiding place was as good as another.

Elephants were stampeding outside her door.

Groaning, Jolie pulled the covers over her head and tried to go back to sleep.

"Kat? Kat? Are you awake? Let me in."

Good grief, it was Elizabeth, up at the crack of… Jolie glanced at the clock. Ten?

Throwing back the covers, she raced to open the door. Elizabeth looked like somebody who had just come from a Miss America competition, daytime-wear segment.

Jolie glanced over to see if Lance might be coming out of or going into his bedroom, then felt both miffed and relieved not to see him.

"I have to talk to you, Kat."

"Can I listen from the bed? I'm beat."

"Poor baby. All that cooking."

"Yeah, well." Jolie got under her covers, then patted the mattress. "Sit. Tell all."

Elizabeth laughed. "As if last night didn't *tell all*."

"Well, it did give me a hint or two. You like this man, don't you?"

"Like him?" Elizabeth pushed her beautiful hair back from her gorgeous face. "I'm falling in love with him."

The green-eyed monster reared its ugly head, but Jolie beat it back. She was happy for her sister. She really was.

"From the looks of things, he loves you right back."

"Amazing, isn't it?"

"Why? You're the world's greatest catch and he's...well, he's a hunk."

"He's sweet and funny and big-hearted and...." Elizabeth flopped back against the pillows and sighed. "Gosh, Kat, I never dreamed I'd fall for a man like him."

"Why wouldn't you want a sweet, funny, big-hearted man?"

"You know what I mean. He's not at all my type. He's...macho and drop-dead sexy and... My goodness, Kat, he's the kind of man some women call a hunk."

"I just did." Did that put her in the suspicious category Elizabeth called "some women?" What were her other less-than-sterling attributes? she wondered.

"Oh, Kat." Elizabeth raised up on her elbow to look at her sister. "I didn't mean that the way it sounded. I'm so giddy I hardly know what I'm saying."

Elizabeth? Giddy? Would wonders never cease?

"That's okay," Jolie said. "You're entitled."

"It's not like me to go off the deep end like this. I mean…my gosh, Kat, I've just met him."

"You've known him for ten years."

"Technically. I know Josh has talked about him a lot, but I've only seen him a couple of times. Why didn't I fall for him then?"

Elizabeth rolled up on her elbow once more, and if Jolie had seen a real doubt in her face, she'd have tried to talk her big sister out of the notion that she loved an almost-stranger. What she saw was radiance and a clear certainty that, for some reason, made Jolie want to cry.

"Of course, it's much too soon, but after all, I'm thirty-five years old!"

"This is not about age, is it?"

"No. Lord, no. I'm just saying that if I don't have sense enough to make smart decisions by now, I never will."

"Nobody would ever call you anything but

smart.'' Jolie grinned at her. ''Except Michael, and he calls you *Lizzie*.''

Elizabeth made a face of mock horror, then grinned. ''Music to my ears. *Irish* music.''

Chapter Thirteen

By the time Jolie and her sister got downstairs it
was eleven o'clock. Aunt Kitty and Josh were in the
library playing checkers, and Michael was thumbing
through one of Lucy's romance novels while he
waited for Elizabeth. Lance was nowhere in sight.

"Good morning, dears." Aunt Kitty got up from
her board game to hug Jolie and Elizabeth. Patting
Jolie's face, she said, "You look tired."

"I couldn't sleep last night."

"Any reason?"

She wasn't about to go into reasons. Instead she
said, "Oh, my gosh, look at the time. I've got to get
to the airport to pick up Mother, Ben and Aunt
Dolly."

"Michael and I are going to do that," Elizabeth said, then swished out of the house with her besotted Irishman.

Why couldn't Lance look at Jolie like that? Shoot, why couldn't he even stick around to look at her, period?

She slumped into a wing chair and watched while Josh and Aunt Kitty finished their game.

"Here, Kat," Aunt Kitty said. "Take my place. I'm going out to the garden. I think some sprigs of rosemary would smell nice in here."

Jolie's heart wasn't into checkers, and Josh knew it.

"Looking for somebody, Kat?"

She didn't even consider trying to fool Josh. As a minister, he was in the business of seeing through facades to his parishioners' innermost souls.

"Yes. Have you seen Lance?"

"Had breakfast with him. Early. He left right after that to go to Pontotoc."

There was only one place he could be: Hanging Grapes Haven. Jolie forgot their misunderstanding and her anger. She forgot everything except Lance's extraordinary kindness to a dear old woman who had no family.

"Josh, if you were getting a present for somebody you really liked, but the other person didn't like you back in the same way, what would you get?"

"It's according to the purpose of your gift."

"What do you mean?"

"Do you want to give Lance a gift because you don't want him to feel left out at Christmas, or do you want something more personal?"

"Personal, definitely. But not socks or gloves. That's so overdone."

"I'll help you." Josh put the board game away. "Let's go shopping, Kat."

Lance played his harmonica for Birdie, helped her select a dress to wear to Christmas dinner the next evening, and helped her name her baby birds, the new glass ornaments he'd brought her. Then she produced Rachel Carson's *Silent Spring* from the nursing home library, and he read to her until the sound of the supper cart outside her door signaled approaching darkness.

He kissed her goodbye, then watched as she stood at the window, waving. It struck him that a woman interested in Rachel Carson's outcry against chemicals that silenced birdsong might have been an ornithologist or, at the very least, a member of the Audubon Society.

On the way back to Shady Grove he stopped to get a gas refill and directions to the nearest big town. He wanted to buy Italian wine for the Christmas dinner, and he wanted to buy a gift for Jolie.

Why not? For the last several days she'd been a lovely hostess to him.

Who are you kidding?

Okay, she'd been more. She *was* more, but that didn't mean he had to buy a diamond.

He found the wine in Tupelo, and also a large sprawling mall. Naturally, the first store was a jeweler's. A square-cut sapphire-and-diamond ring shouted *Jolie,* but he moved on to an office supply store, with only one backward glance. After he left there, a window display at a lingerie boutique snared him. Imagining Jolie's face on all the mannequins, he got trapped by his own libido and had to stand in front of the naughty confections a good while before he could move on.

Resolved to look the other way the next time he saw women's lingerie, he hurried along the crowded corridors filled with last-minute shoppers until he saw a store that suited him. It sold videos and DVDs...and in the window was a cardboard cutout of Jimmy Stewart.

Even with expanded holiday shopping hours, it was almost closing time when Lance went inside. In order to get what he wanted he'd have to do some fast shopping.

And some fast talking.

Jolie thought her mother, Aunt Dolly and Ben would never go to bed. Josh, an early-to-bed, early-to-rise man, had bid them good-night an hour earlier, and Aunt Kitty had gone to bed at eight-thirty.

With Dolly's frequent corrections and additions, and Ben's smiling indulgence, Lucy told Jolie every last detail of everything they'd done in California. Not that Jolie didn't want to hear. She just wished Elizabeth had been there to deflect some of the attention. She and Michael had vanished shortly after dinner, destination unknown.

And where in the world was Lance?

She glanced at the clock. Ten minutes after eleven. Did the nursing home allow you to stay that long?

"Okay," Lucy said. "I can take a hint."

"What hint?"

"Clock watching is a sure sign of boredom. We've bored you to death."

"Speak for yourself, Lucille Coltrane," Aunt Dolly said. "I never bore anybody. I'd be out of a job if I did."

"Trust me, Dolly, you'll never be out of a job," Ben said, and Dolly dramatically blew him a kiss.

"Good Lord, Ben, let's go to bed before I have to kill Dolly for flirting with you." She kissed Jolie. "Good night, dear."

Jolie breathed a sigh of relief when she was alone. Now she could put Lance's gift under the tree without the family asking a million questions.

She retrieved the gift from her bedroom, then went back downstairs and stood beneath the sparkling Christmas lights, remembering how the theft of gifts had brought her and Lance together.

She could hardly bear the thought that Christmas would soon be over and he would be leaving.

She was in the process of putting her gift to him under the tree when she heard footsteps. She turned and there was Lance, filling the doorway, filling her vision, filling her heart.

"Hello, Jolie. I didn't expect to see you here."

His smile took some of the sting out of his words, but they got her dander up, anyway. Maybe it was holiday stress, maybe it was nerves, maybe it was just her geared-for-battle personality.

"Alone, you mean."

"I was out of line about what happened in the kitchen."

"*Nothing* happened in the kitchen."

She wanted to stomp out and never speak to him again, or at least for the next twenty minutes, but he was between her and her bedroom. To make matters worse, he'd caught her red-handed with a gift. Not just any gift, either, but one that had cost her a whole week's worth of groceries.

"I didn't mean to start a fight," he said. "In fact, I'm glad to see you. Wait right here...please."

If he hadn't added "please" she'd have marched past him, spitting fire.

Or maybe not. She could never stay mad at anybody for long. Especially Lance.

When he came back he was bearing gifts, a handful of beautifully wrapped packages, plus a large, unwieldy object.

"I was going to put these under the tree, but since you're here…" He handed her the packages. "Merry Christmas, Jolie."

She started crying. Naturally. Put her in any romantic situation where she wanted to look like Julia Roberts, only blond, and she ended up looking like Rudolph, red nose and all.

Lance pulled his handkerchief out of his pocket. "Here. I know you don't have one."

"You're right." She wiped her face, then blew her nose. "That's me, always unprepared."

"No, you're not. And I want you to stop thinking of yourself that way."

Why? She didn't dare ask. The correct answer would be, *Because I love you.* But what if he didn't say that? She'd only feel worse.

"Okay. I will. I promise." She went to the tree and got his gift. "I have something for you, too. And I'm dying for you to open it."

"You first."

She tore into the wrapping. His first gift was a beautiful hand-tooled leather desk set.

"For that new office you're going to have," he told her, and she had to use his handkerchief again. She was never going to be able to get the mascara out.

"This is wonderful." She traced the design on the

soft leather. The desk set was more than a gift; it was an affirmation. Lance believed in her. "It's the best gift I ever had. Thank you, Lance."

"You're welcome."

She wished she could kiss him, or at least hug him, but his face, his entire body language said, *Keep off.* Pulling her gaze away, she tore open the next package.

It was a DVD of the two Jimmy Stewart movies they'd watched—or tried to—at the drive-in. Did that mean he wanted her to remember that night? Did two sentimental movies spell *love?*

"Everybody ought to have copies of those two classics," he said.

She tried to read romance into his words, but couldn't. Maybe a bit of nostalgia and just a hint of hope. Or was she being foolishly sentimental?

"I have something for you, too...." She bit her lower lip. Only a foolish woman would let her heart show when there seemed no hope of reciprocity. What the heck. She was a foolish woman.

She put the gift in his hand and added, "Because...you mean the world to me."

His big warm hand closed around hers, and his dark eyes captured hers with a look that she would remember till she was on her deathbed.

"And you to me."

She would have closed her eyes and drowned in

his deep voice, but she didn't want to miss seeing him for a single second.

For a heart-stopping eternity she thought he was going to kiss her; she thought she'd broken past all his barriers and found the warm, loving heart he was reserving just for her. But no, he released her hand and opened his gift.

The harmonica she'd given him was top of the line. She'd had no idea you could pay that much for something so small. But the look on his face was worth it. His joy was pure and absolute.

He inspected the blues harp, ran his fingers over the smooth surface, put it to his mouth and played a riff. Even if she never saw him again, she would remember him with his lips caressing the gift she had given him.

"Key of G. How did you know?"

Josh had told her. He and Lance had talked about music over breakfast, specifically the fact that Lance's G harmonica was about shot.

"It's a secret, and a wise woman never reveals her secrets."

"I'll bet you'd tell Jimmy Stewart."

"Of course I would. I would walk over water for Jimmy Stewart."

How easy it was to laugh with Lance. Why couldn't it be that easy to love with him?

He picked up the unwieldy cardboard, which

turned out to be a life-size cutout of her all-time-favorite actor.

"Start walking."

She walked around her cardboard movie idol, admired him from all angles, bowed to him, then kissed his stiff face and giggled.

"I *love* him. I've seen one just like him at Brooks Music and Video Store at the mall in Tupelo, but he wasn't for sale."

"He's one and the same."

"How in the world did you get him?"

"You have your secrets, I have mine."

"He's perfect. The perfect man, the strong silent type, always available, always smiling." Unable to restrain herself any longer, she threw her arms around Lance. "Oh, thank you."

He held her so close she could feel the strong beating of his heart against her own. She wanted to stay there forever.

"You're…special to me, Jolie." He was still holding her close. "You're good for me. I've laughed more in the last few days than I have in years."

People always laughed around her. Kat the clown. But wasn't that a good trait to have—the ability to evoke joy? Seeing herself through Lance's eyes, she was beginning to understand that what she needed was not a complete overhaul, but a little fine tuning.

"You're good for me, too." And oh, he was still holding her close. Even if he left tomorrow and she never saw him again, she would always be grateful for having known him. She would always remember the Christmas she'd found true love.

She pressed her cheek against his heart.

He held her that way for a long time, but when she felt the stirrings in her body and his, he stepped back.

"Jolie, when you look at Jimmy Stewart I want you to remember what you told me—that you would walk on water for him. You can do anything you want to, and when you doubt your own abilities, do it for Jimmy.

"And do it for me," Lance whispered, running his knuckles softly down her cheek.

All she could do was nod, because if she said a single word she was going to start crying again.

He leaned down and kissed her softly on the lips. "Good night, Jolie. Merry Christmas."

"You, too," she said, but he was already on the way out the door.

She waited until the sound of his footsteps faded, then she said, "Well, Jimmy, I guess it's just you and me."

Chapter Fourteen

Jolie's alarm jerked her out of a dream where she and Jimmy Stewart were honeymooning in Tahiti, and into the reality of her Big Cooking Debut. She crawled out of bed and came face-to-face with her cardboard man.

"I know you wanted a little hanky-panky under the sheets this morning, but I have too much to do. Some other time, huh?" she whispered.

Dressing quickly in jeans and a T-shirt, she crept through the still-sleeping household to the kitchen. As she reached for the light, a familiar voice said, "Good morning, sleepyhead."

His rich, sexy, morning voice nearly made her

swoon. She held on to the door frame and gave a big yawn so he'd think she was so sleepy she could hardly hold herself upright.

"Lance…what in the world are you doing sitting here in the dark? And at this god-awful hour?"

"I made coffee."

"I see that. But why?"

"This is your big day. I came to lend moral support."

It was on the tip of her tongue to say, "You mean, to clean up my messes?" but she bit her tongue. Starting today she was going to be confident and self-assured and efficient.

And if she made any messes, heaven forbid, she'd clean them up herself.

"Then stand back and watch a master chef at work," she told him, and he laughed.

"Good girl."

Taking a deep breath, Jolie put aside memories of charred biscuits and smoking bacon, then attacked the Christmas dinner with a vengeance. At first she was achingly aware of Lance sitting on a bar stool sipping coffee and watching her. Gradually, though, she grew comfortable with his quiet presence.

Around eight, Aunt Kitty came in and said, "What can I do to help?"

"Keep everybody out," Jolie said. "I have it under control."

"Why don't I grab juice and cereal fixings and set

up breakfast in the sunroom?'' her aunt said. ''It's going to be a beautiful day.''

Her prediction turned out to be true. Around noon Matt arrived with his pregnant wife, Sandi, and their adorable little adopted girl, big-eyed over her first Christmas in America. Lance left at two to get Birdie, while Elizabeth drifted in and out of the kitchen to check on things, always with Michael at her side.

At three Lucy said, ''Kat, darling, you're going to wear yourself out. We'll all pitch in and help you finish.''

''No, thank you, Mother. I have to do this by myself.''

Turning to her companion and long-time friend, Lucy said, ''Ben, do something.'' And he came around the cooking island to massage Jolie's neck.

About that time Lance appeared in the doorway and said, ''Why don't I take over here and let you folks enjoy the fire Josh built?''

Ben and Lucy left, and suddenly Lance, big and dark and gorgeous, was the one massaging her shoulders, smelling of fresh air and the clean scent of soap that was as familiar to Jolie as her own breath. It was amazing the difference a pair of hands could make.

Ben's hands had eased the ache across her shoulders. Lance's lit little fires under her skin and sent shivers through her.

''Umm,'' she said. ''That is so wonderful.''

''Yes, it is.''

She leaned back against him, the great solid warmth of his chest and the long, strong length of his legs. And she forgot everything except the desire that arced between them.

Lord, had she already put the garlic seasoning in the pasta salad? And what about the capers?

She managed to murmur, "The salad," but she hadn't the least interest in pasta or Christmas feasts or even a houseful of family watching to see whether she succeeded or failed.

With one hand still on her neck, Lance reached over and added capers, then deftly dumped in the garlic. With her heart already in her throat, she couldn't speak. She couldn't do anything except stand there with her legs turning to butter.

His hands were in her hair now, just at the base of her neck, and that *thing* he was doing made her wish for Lance in her bedroom, instead of Jimmy Stewart.

Yeah, when pigs fly.

In a few hours he would be gone. And suddenly there were a million things she wanted to say to him.

"Better now?" he asked.

"Umm," was all she could manage. Oh, Lord, he was going to go back to his bar stool, and her golden opportunity would be lost forever. "Lance…"

She turned to face him and her words flew right out of her head. He was gazing at her in that take-no-prisoners way that meant he was going to kiss her…and kiss her thoroughly.

Her last coherent thought was *What if somebody comes in?* and then it didn't matter. The entire family could traipse through the kitchen for all she cared. Jolie was in a picture-perfect world where the girl meets the man of her dreams and the man gets the girl.

Oh, if only it were so.

This man would never take a woman lightly. He would never offer a one-night stand, a love 'em and leave 'em proposition. With Lancelot Estes, it would be all or nothing at all.

Like his namesake, he was a warrior to the bone, and warriors' promises were never broken. Their code of honor didn't allow it.

There would be no pretty, shallow words from him. When he made up his mind, he would act with a swiftness and certainty that would leave no doubt about his intentions.

Jolie was vaguely aware of the kitchen door opening, then closing again. She was vaguely aware of the tick of the art deco clock on the wall. And she was totally, vividly aware of Lance's lips locked on hers, his body pressed so close there wasn't room for so much as a broom straw between them.

Don't let it end.

But it did. He eased back, and the space between them felt two miles wide.

She touched her kiss-swollen lips, smoothed her damp hair back from her face.

"I never did say thank you for everything you've done for me, Lance."

"You just did." He put his hand to her cheek and looked so deeply into her eyes she was certain he would start kissing her again. He wanted to. She could see it.

"Jolie, I'll be leaving as soon as dinner is over."

"I thought you might."

"This is goodbye."

"I know." She forced a smile. "I guess it's appropriate to say goodbye in the kitchen, since this is where we met."

"Yes." He captured her eyes again with a long, intense gaze that stole her breath and threatened to topple her reason.

I am in love with this man. The truth wasn't sudden, but something Jolie had refused to acknowledge until she had to say goodbye.

He was going God only knew where, and she was going back to Memphis in hot pursuit of a new job. She'd just have to get over it, that was all.

Would she ever see him again? Did he hear her heart breaking?

"I'll be coming back to Pontotoc from time to time to check on Birdie." Did he read minds, in addition to all his many other talents? "And Jolie... I *will* see you again. That's a promise."

All she could do was nod, while she stored his promise in her heart and held on tight.

The oven timer went off and Lance grabbed pot holders, then took the turkey out of the oven. It was the most scrumptious looking bird they'd ever had for Christmas. And she'd done it all by herself.

She'd made a plan and stuck to it.

With a little help from a temporary knight in shining armor.

She beamed at him. "We did it."

"No. You did it." He gave her one last, long look, then said, "I'd better go check on Birdie. See you at dinner."

She watched until the door swung shut behind him, then stood in the middle of the kitchen trying to work up enough enthusiasm to haul herself up the stairs and put on some festive clothes.

"Kat?" Elizabeth came in looking like a princess in blue velvet. "I'm sorry about the interruption earlier."

"That was you?"

"Yes. I guess I owed you one."

Jolie joined her sister's laughter, though she definitely wasn't in the mood.

"Before you go upstairs to change, there's something I have to tell you," her sister said, as if the stars in her eyes didn't say it all. "Michael asked me to marry him, and I said yes."

Elizabeth took her silence for concern, which was

fine by Jolie. She *was·*concerned. But not seriously.
Her big sister never made mistakes, and she wasn't
likely to start now.

"I realize this is hasty, but believe me, I'm certain,
and so is he."

"I'm so happy for you." Jolie hugged her sister.

"And I'm happy for you, too." Elizabeth sur-
veyed the huge array of food. "Just look at all this.
You did it, Kat. You really did it. I'm so proud of
you."

"Are you going to announce your engagement at
dinner?"

"No. You're the star of the show tonight. After
all this hard work you deserve the limelight, and I
intend to see that you get it." Elizabeth donned a bib
apron. "Go on upstairs and get gorgeous. Michael's
coming down in a minute and we'll set the table."

"Thanks." She was at the door when her sister
added, "I might even do a documentary about
women like your friend Birdie, the forgotten souls
who fall through the cracks of society...unless
they're lucky enough to be rescued by someone like
you."

Jolie started to add "and Lance," but she didn't.
Her heart was still too raw to speak his name.

"I'm the lucky one."

Lance got through dinner. He didn't know how.
Jolie was wearing a soft blue sweater that made him

itch to touch her. Instead of staring, he listened to the ebb and flow of conversation, much of it compliments on Jolie's cooking. The only time he ever looked directly at her was when she opened her mouth to disclaim credit for the feast.

He squelched her confessions with one look. She deserved the glory and he intended to see that she got it.

Lucy announced that dessert and coffee would be served in the living room, and he watched until Jolie disappeared down the hall with Birdie in tow.

It was time to go. He'd already thanked his hostess and said his private goodbyes to Birdie and Jolie. Now the only person he had to see was Elizabeth.

Catching his eye, she lingered until the others had left the room. "I want to thank you for sharing your family Christmas."

She put her hand on his arm. "Did you enjoy it? Really?"

"Yes." More than she'd ever know. "Elizabeth, this thing between you and Sullivan seems to be moving pretty fast. Be careful."

"Oh, Lance." He'd always thought the prettiest thing about Elizabeth was her laughter. It pealed like bells through the empty dining room. "He's a pussycat. And he thinks you're terrific."

"He doesn't know me."

"Yes, he does. Don't get mad. I didn't tell, and he won't tell, either. He recognized your name from the papers. He said, and I quote, 'He's a damn hero, and if the public doesn't realize that, they ought to be ashamed'.''

''Tell him I'll shake his hand the next time I see him.''

''When will that be, Lance?''

''I don't know.'' He had a name to discover and dragons to slay. Leaning down, he kissed her cheek. ''Take care of yourself, beautiful.''

''You too, hotshot.''

Chapter Fifteen

"I don't understand why you're leaving today," Lucy said.

"After I take Miss Birdie to Pontotoc I want to get back to Memphis so I can spend the rest of the holidays spiffing up my apartment," Jolie told her.

"You're not upset because I'm going to marry Ben, are you?"

Lucy and Ben had announced their intentions the previous night during dessert and coffee.

"Good heavens, Mother. I'm thrilled. And so are Elizabeth and Matt. You two deserve some happiness."

"We are perfectly happy with our unconventional

lifestyle, but it doesn't make sense to keep two houses.... You'll come back for the New Year's Eve party, won't you?''

The last thing she wanted to do was come back to O'Banyon Manor to witness the rest of her family happily paired off, each with somebody to love. Still, Lucy was looking so hopeful that Jolie couldn't bear to disappoint her.

''I'll see,'' she answered, all the while thinking she'd find some excuse not to come. Unless, of course, Elizabeth decided to announce *her* engagement.

Jolie kissed her mother's cheek. '''Bye, Mom. I'll call you when I get home.''

She packed her car, then set off to Hanging Grapes Haven with Birdie in the front seat and Jimmy Stewart in the back.

''Is that Jacky?'' Birdie asked.

''No, that's just a cardboard cutout.''

''Why is he grinning like that? Does he know something we don't?''

Obviously, this was not one of Birdie's good days. Jolie decided to just go with the flow.

''Probably,'' she said.

''Well, he ought to let us in on the joke.''

Jolie wished *somebody* would. Birdie swiveled around and spent the remainder of the drive talking to Jimmy Stewart.

If there was any way she could take care of Birdie,

Jolie would have just taken her to Memphis, but that was out of the question. She didn't have enough space, and she didn't have the financial resources. Besides, who would look after Birdie while Jolie worked?

She said goodbye, then made the long, lonely drive home. When she got back to Memphis she pulled a double fistful of Christmas cards out of her mailbox. She was so grateful to the U.S. Post Office she thought she might write them a thank-you note. Most of her friends sent long newsletters, especially the married ones. Now she'd have something to do tonight instead of sitting around talking to Jimmy Stewart and missing Lance.

Ina's call came while Lance was on his way to Atlanta. He was sitting in a diner on the Alabama-Georgia border when his cell phone rang.

"I'm so glad I caught you," his former house-mother said. "I have news."

"Good news, I hope."

"Not exactly. The little cookie girl called Sarah, the one I thought might be your mother, died the year after I left the orphanage. I'm sorry, Lancelot."

"You did all you could, and I'm grateful."

"She does have family, though—a younger brother still living in Phoenix, if that helps."

"Yes. If you'll give me the address I'd like to come out and talk to him."

"Don't you dare come without stopping by to visit me. Do you have a pen and pencil handy?"

Lance wrote down the address, thinking a phone call would be easier, but a trip to Phoenix would help fill up the remainder of his holiday. Even better, it would put more than a thousand miles between him and Jolie, and remove all temptation to drive up to Memphis to see her. There was no way he could see her again without making love with her, and no way he would make love with her until he had a name and a promise to go with it.

During the last three days Jolie had spent so much time organizing her apartment, she dreamed about alphabetized cans of soup. When somebody knocked and she saw her neighbor Connie through the peephole, she was so grateful she pulled her friend inside, then danced a jig.

"Is this happiness to see me?" Connie asked.

"You bet it is. I didn't expect you back until after the first."

"Changed my mind. Couldn't wait to show off this." She held up a finger adorned with a diamond ring. "Besides, company and fish stink after three days. I think Wayne's parents were as tired of me as I was of them."

Jolie couldn't take her eyes off the diamond. Was everybody in the world getting married? What was it—something in the water? Something in the air?

Obviously, she was immune.

For the first time in her life she had to force enthusiasm for Connie's good fortune. "That's great. It really is. I'm so happy for you. I really am."

"Oh, yeah? You don't sound happy. What's up?"

Jolie ticked off the reasons on her fingers. "My job's still hanging. I met a man I love but I don't think he feels the same. And mops with those little screw-on sponges ought to be outlawed."

"Last time I used one I wrapped duct tape around the sponge to hold it on. By the way, your apartment looks great, and I don't think you're going to hear from the SPCA until after the first. Now tell *all.*"

"There's nothing to tell, except a few kisses that were over-the-moon wonderful."

"Listen, Kat, if you felt those kinds of sparks, you can bet he felt something."

"How do you know?"

"Rule number five in the Good Girl's Book of Love—if sparks are flying, both parties feel them."

"I've never heard of that book."

"I just made it up. But it's true. Trust me. Every man I kissed felt flat till Wayne Humphries lit my fire. He said it was the same with him."

"Connie, do you think I can make myself over and get a new job and be in love all at the same time?"

"Why not? That's what the women's magazines tell us—we're supposed to have it all."

"Tomorrow, will you go down to Saint John's and light a candle with me?"

"I thought you were Methodist."

"It won't hurt to cover all the bases."

Lance's flight out of Atlanta was delayed, so it was nearly midnight when he reached Phoenix, far too late to call the man Ina had told him about.

He made the call first thing the next morning. Lance had the distinct feeling that the man might have refused to see him—a stranger calling out of the blue—if he hadn't already flown across the country.

Lance rented a four-wheel-drive truck, then wound his way into the red bluffs until he came to a ranch on the outskirts of town. The wooden sign over the curved entranceway read Shane Ranch.

The man he was going to see, Sarah's younger brother, was a member of the Apache Nation. Lance had learned that from Ina, as well as the fact that Clyde Shane was an influential man, greatly respected in his community. Lance could see why he wouldn't welcome the idea of anyone coming in to lay claim to the family.

On the other hand, this could turn into a wild-goose chase. Maybe Sarah Shane was not Lance's mother. Even if she was, the family might have its reasons for keeping the birth a secret.

Lance parked his rental truck beside a Porsche and

two Cadillacs, then went through a winding rock garden complete with waterfall, and rang the doorbell of the sprawling cypress-wood house.

A tall, dark-skinned man with the eyes of a warrior opened the door.

"Lancelot Estes?"

"Yes."

"Come in. I have a luncheon meeting at noon, so we'll make this brief."

"I understand."

He led Lance into an office that had only one personal touch: a framed photograph of a pretty, dark-eyed woman with gray in her hair. Probably his wife. There was nothing else to give Lance a clue about the man.

He had told Clyde that he was looking for his birth mother and that he had reason to believe Sarah might be the one, so he didn't waste time repeating it. Instead, he sat in a leather wing chair facing the desk and waited for his host to speak.

"What information do you have that led you to me?" he asked.

"It's anecdotal. Sarah used to sell cookies at the orphanage where I grew up, and my friend, who was housemother at that time, believes Sarah's interest in me was personal."

"You have nothing, then."

"No. Nothing concrete. Only instincts, which I never discount. I'm an agent with the International

Security Force, Mr. Shane. My survival often depends on my instincts."

"My sister Sarah died of leukemia at the age of twenty-one, Mr. Estes. She was not married and she had no children." Clyde Shane stood up. "I'm sorry you've come all this way."

The meeting was over. "Thank you for your time, Mr. Shane." Lance put his card on the desk. "If you think of anything that might help me find my birth mother, please call."

As he walked down the hall beside the taciturn man, his training as well as his instincts kicked into high gear. Clyde Shane was lying. All the signs were there: his failure to look directly at Lance, the rapid blinking when he talked about Sarah, the change of pitch in his voice.

Still, Lance had no choice but to leave. He had no concrete evidence, and even if he did, he couldn't force this man to tell him the truth. No crime had been committed. No laws broken.

He was back at square one. He would have changed his ticket and flown back to Atlanta tomorrow if he hadn't promised to visit Ina. Lance never broke a promise, and he wasn't going to start now.

Even a man without a name could still have honor.

Elizabeth called Jolie at the Pampered Pooch Salon, her Tuesday and Thursday client. Mondays and

Wednesdays Jolie groomed at Pretty Pets. Fridays and weekends she picked up jobs at dog shows.

"I didn't interrupt anything, did I, Kat?"

Jolie brushed dog hair off her smock and blew her bangs out of her eyes. Lord, her hair grew like a weed.

"Nothing that can't wait till my favorite soap opera gets Bo and Hope back together."

"Listen, I'm not announcing my engagement at Mother's New Year's Eve party."

"Well, okay. When are you announcing it?"

"Never! The engagement is off!"

"But I thought you were madly in love."

"*Mad* is the operative word here. I must have been insane to get mixed up with that...that Irish hooligan."

"What happened?"

"I flew up to Boston right after Christmas, to meet his family."

"And?"

"There are so *many* of them! They kept inspecting me like I'm a brood cow and saying, 'Now, how old are you?' And when I told them thirty-five, they said, 'You and Michael will want to get started on the family right away.' They actually thought I was going to give up my career and settle down in Podunksville to raise babies."

"But you want children, don't you?"

"That's not the point."

"What is the point?"

"Michael just laughed. I wanted to kill him."

"That's all? That's the reason you broke up with him?"

"That's not the half of it! Once the beer got flowing, his brother Thomas wanted Michael to take off his shirt and show how many places he'd been shot. God, he could die on me!"

Elizabeth started crying, and Jolie figured the world was coming to an end, because her sister never cried.

"I'm sure everything will work out." Jolie really believed what she told her sister, because the fact was, things always *did* work out for Elizabeth.

"I don't want to see him again." Her sister sniffled. "You won't tell Mom any of this, will you, Kat?"

"Not even if restless natives stick thorns under my fingernails."

"Thanks. Have you talked to Lance?"

"No." It was a painful admission that made her sound like a girl nobody wanted to love. "Why?"

"I was going to discuss the documentary with him…about forgotten seniors. He's not returning my calls, but that's not unusual. I want to interview him about Birdie. You, too, Kat."

It was amazing how Elizabeth could bounce back from a crisis. Jolie wished she could be more like that.

"Can you wait till my bangs grow out? They would scare old ladies and little children."

"Listen, if Lance calls, tell him to call me ASAP, okay? I want to start this ball rolling while the idea is hot."

"I will," Jolie answered. She wasn't about to admit that chances of the moon turning to cheese were greater than those of Lance calling her.

She couldn't worry about that now. She had too many other things on her mind. Mrs. Jenkins's poodle, for one. She'd developed the nervous habit of gnawing her hair off in wads, and it was Jolie's job to make her beautiful again.

She picked up her clippers and went back to her grooming room. "Are you ready for this, Isadora?" The dog licked her hands. "Okay, then, let's get beautiful."

Jolie glared at the cell phone, muttering, "Ring, why don't you?" then finally put it on the bookshelf within easy reach…just in case.

Chapter Sixteen

Once Jolie convinced her mother that she wouldn't die of loneliness because she wasn't driving down to Mississippi for the New Year's Eve party, she called to check on Birdie. Then she spent the next half hour trying to decide between an exciting evening with Harry Potter or an uplifting one with Jimmy Stewart. Harry Potter won. Putting on her long wool coat and hat because a sudden dip in temperature plus the threat of snow had surprised and chilled Memphis residents, Jolie went to the movies.

Okay, so maybe she wouldn't get kissed at midnight, but she got to eat a large bucket of buttered popcorn all by herself. It was one of the many joys of being single. Jolie couldn't think of the others right now because her heart hurt a little, but she was sure she would think of them tomorrow. After all, tomorrow was the start of a brand-new year.

She was the only person who cried at the Harry Potter movie, but that wasn't saying much because there were only two other people in the theater. Didn't they have any sensitivity?

Sitting in the dark, her fingers greasy with butter and her face streaked with tears, Jolie made a mental note to head to Memphis State University as soon as the holidays were over and register for Spanish classes, never mind that it was Elizabeth's choice. Her sister was right. Spanish made more sense.

Elizabeth always made sense, and look what it had gotten her: success, financial security and a fiancé who dropped out of the blue and into her arms. Well, strike the fiancé. At least for now. Still, Jolie would do well to pattern herself after her sister. Heck, maybe she'd even call Elizabeth tomorrow and ask to borrow her New Year's resolutions. It couldn't hurt.

But the next day, thoughts of calling her sister flew right out of her mind, when the gift shop around the corner delivered a box of chocolates with a note attached: "Happy New Year, Jolie."

It was signed simply "Lance," and though it wasn't a declaration of love, it was enough. For now.

* * *

Two weeks after he'd left O'Banyon Manor, Lance headed back again, this time to be interviewed. Appearing on film was the next to last thing he wanted to do right now. The last thing was to see Jolie. He wasn't ready. But Elizabeth had asked a favor, and he hadn't been reassigned yet, so how could he say no after she'd so generously invited him to share her family's Christmas?

The closer he got to Shady Grove the more tense he became. Keeping his hands off Jolie had been difficult before. After a three-week separation, it was going to be next to impossible. He was almost in sight of O'Banyon Manor when he decided he'd visit Birdie first. The short detour wouldn't delay Elizabeth's filming, but it would postpone facing Jolie.

Even though he called Birdie two times a week, nothing could replace personal visits. Besides seeing her, he needed the staff to see *him.* He wanted them to know that somebody was watching on Birdie's behalf, somebody who cared.

Halfway to Pontotoc the rains started and the temperature tumbled. If it kept dropping, the roads could get bad, and nobody in the South was equipped to deal with ice-slick roads, including Lance. But he decided to push on. He could hole up at a motel if road conditions got bad enough.

When he pulled into the nursing home's parking lot, the first thing he saw was Jolie's car with the still-dented fender. It was too late to go back now. Rain was already freezing on the roads. Besides, if he didn't get in there pronto, Jolie would probably set out for home and end up in a ditch again. Or worse.

He heard the Christmas music before he got to Birdie's room. "Jingle Bell Rock" blared while Birdie and Jolie danced. The sight made his heart hurt. He watched from the doorway until Jolie spotted him.

"Lance. How wonderful to see you." Her voice was full of smiles and music, and it thawed him right down to the bone.

"You, too, Jolie. How have you been? How's the bruise?"

"Great…and all gone." She pushed her bangs off her forehead like a little girl. He wanted to hug her.

"Good," he said, then tore himself loose from her spell and caught Birdie in a bear hug.

"Jacky! Shame on you for missing all the fun. Jolie and I have been dancing."

"So I see." He glanced around the room for the fruit basket he'd sent earlier in the week. Her Christmas tree was still up, the faux bird's nests were still scattered about the room, but the basket was nowhere in sight. Since she seemed to be in good mind, he asked, "Did you get the fruit basket I sent?"

"That poor Mr. Williams down the hall doesn't

have a soul to his name. I told him, You take this. I've got my birds, and I've got my friends.''

''I'll send you another.''

Birdie grinned. ''I bet he'll like that one, too.''

''Lance, I have something to show you.'' Jolie pulled a yellowed envelope out of an ancient copy of *Gone With the Wind.* Inside was a newspaper account of a train wreck that had killed Jack Garcy and his son, Jack, Jr., more than thirty years ago. They were survived by Burdine Garcy.

''She asked me to read to her, then dug this book out from the bottom of her closet. So now we know.''

Birdie put her hand on Lance's arm anxiously. ''Jacky?''

''It's all right.'' He put his arms around her. ''You can call me Jacky. I'll be your son.''

Jolie teared up as she drifted toward the window, trailing a cloud of perfume that stole his reason. ''Oh, no,'' she said. ''Just look out there. I'd better head back before the weather gets any worse.''

''The roads are already too bad to drive home. There's a motel less than a mile away. We'll take your car. I'll drive.''

''But I can't…we can't….''

''Separate rooms, Jolie.''

They got separate rooms, much to Jolie's relief. Who was she kidding? Much to her disappointment was more like it.

It was only nine o'clock, and she'd had to eat in the dining room all by herself because Lance had been on the road all day and said he would order room service. Now she was sitting here looking at four walls, with nothing on television but reruns of the *Golden Girls,* and what was she supposed to do? Chew her fingernails down to the quick? Count the fringe on the tacky shag carpet? Die of unrequited love?

The world's most desirable man was just beyond the connecting door and she couldn't think of a single reason to knock.

Hi, do you want to put your arms around me and kiss me till I swoon? Actually, she wanted more.

Hello, would you like to come into my bed and help me muss the covers? That was more like it, but didn't most men revel in the chase?

Hi, do you want to come in and play with me? Okay, she was down to the nitty-gritty now, but he hadn't indicated in any way that she still lit his fire...if she ever had.

Hi, do you want to come in and play cards?

That might fly. Believe it or not, she had a deck in her purse, mostly to have at the laundromat while she waited for her clothes to dry, but more often than not to while away evenings in her apartment while Connie and every other red-blooded girl in America had fun with a significant other.

Jolie jumped off the bed, then smoothed the covers so Lance wouldn't think she had a devious agenda. She rummaged in her purse until she found an old lipstick that would probably turn orange on her. It would have to do. Anything was better than pale and unprepared to dazzle.

She knocked on his door, and when he immediately said, "Yes?" she nearly jumped out of her skin. Had he been standing right on the other side? Had he been waiting for her to knock? Thinking about knocking himself?

The connecting door swung wide, and there he was, the man who knocked her socks off.

"Is anything wrong?"

Jolie wanted to stamp her foot. Why was it, every time he saw her, he wanted to fix her problem? Why couldn't she be the kind of woman who left a man speechless with wonder and desire?

"Do you want to play cards?" From the look on his face, you'd think she had just invited him to chop wood on the back forty. She inched away like one of those worms she used to find on the sidewalk in the hot summertime after a rain. "You probably don't even play cards...how silly of me...I'll just..." She waved her hand aimlessly toward the television. "...watch a rerun of *I Love Lucy* or something."

"Jolie...I'd love to play cards with you."

"You would?"

"Yes." He came through the door and she was amazed at how much space he took. Suddenly there was nowhere she could turn without bumping into some delectable-looking part of him.

"But I warn you," he added. "I play to win."

"You've got a tough battle ahead, mister. So do I."

"Good. Make it hard for me."

Oh, my Lord. Naturally, he hadn't meant that the way she took it. She'd better get her mind settled on a higher plane before she embarrassed herself by ripping off her clothes and yelling, "Take me, I'm yours."

"I'll just, um, get the, uh…" She started to get the cards, but first she had to get past him because her purse had spitefully migrated to the far corner of the room just to test her willpower.

Her arm brushed his in passing and the electric shock temporarily paralyzed her. He didn't make matters a bit easier because he was looking at her as if she were a tasty morsel he planned to nibble on.

Lordy, when had that magical transformation taken place? And why?

It must be her lipstick. That was it. He wasn't used to seeing her with painted lips. A little cosmetic enhancement probably added the right touch of pizzazz to rev his motor and set him to salivating.

"Excuse me," she said, then nearly fainted when he leaned down and put his index finger on her lips.

"You have a smear of lipstick...right there."

Did she want to crawl in a hole, or what?

"Thank you."

"You're welcome."

She fled to the far corner of the room and spent three times longer than necessary searching her purse for the deck of cards and going into a near panic. Suddenly, she realized that the no-frills motel offered only the rudiments of comfort—a bed, a chair, a cheap bedside table and a television swung from the ceiling on one of those contraptions they used in hospitals.

There was only one place to play games, cards or otherwise—the bed. Jolie stood with her back to him, trying to keep her naughty thoughts to herself. She wasn't much of an actress. Shoot, she wasn't an actress at all. The minute she turned around he'd know exactly what she was thinking.

"Jolie? Is anything wrong?"

Caught. She'd have to turn around sometime this century.

"Oh, yes. I just realized we don't have any place to play."

Did her glee show? She couldn't tell by looking at him; his face was a mask.

"We'll play on the bed."

If she fainted, would that be a sure sign he drove

her crazy, wild with love? Oh, Lordy. She was crazy about this man. A wicked little fairy had decided to complicate her life by sprinkling I-want-a-white-satin-gown-and-babies-and-a-house-with-a-mortgage dust when she wasn't looking.

The only problem was all those fantasies required a man who loved you right back, and if she thought the one standing in her motel room was going to whisk her off to the chapel of love, she was sadly mistaken.

When In Doubt, Be Bold.

"Okay." She flopped onto the bed as if she had never thought of it as a gateway to paradise. "Let's play. I'll shuffle."

She tried to concentrate on the feel of cards in her hands, the whirring sound they made. Instead she was vividly aware of Lance sitting on the bed. Her breath sawed through her lungs, her skin became sensitized and goose pimply, and heat stung every part of her body.

"Cut." She handed the cards to him, and even the smallest touch—his fingers brushing her hand—heightened the sensations that swept through her.

If she didn't get her mind on the game, she was going down in flaming defeat, *flaming* being the operative word. Trying to focus, she caught her tongue between her teeth. A sudden electric silence forced her to look at him.

He sizzled with pure lust. Had somebody else

come into the room while she wasn't looking? Was a *Playboy* centerfold standing behind her?

"Please, Jolie. Don't do that."

His voice was raw with desire. She could hardly breathe.

"Do what?"

"That thing you do with your tongue."

"Oh...sorry."

"No, don't apologize. It's not you. It's me."

Caught in a web of desire, they stared at each other, the cards forgotten on the bed. Sounds magnified—their breathing, the drip of a leaky faucet in the bathroom, the sleet hitting the window outside. Thoughts outgrew their minds and paraded around the room, shouting for attention.

I want you. I need you. Nothing matters except the passion we can't contain.

"Damn it." Lance raked the cards off the bed and they scattered like frightened children. "I can't do this."

Excited beyond anything she'd ever known, she licked her lips. "Do what?" she whispered.

"Be alone in this bedroom with you."

"It's okay." She touched his hand, and he jerked back as if he'd been gut-punched.

"No. I have nothing to offer. All I can do is take."

A haunted, driven man looked at her, conflicted by dark mysteries and passion.

If I've ever been wise, let it be now.

Slowly she got off the bed and pulled her sweater over her head. She heard his sharp intake of breath. He was watching her, as still and imposing as a mountain. Without taking her eyes off his, she unzipped her jeans and let them slide to the floor.

"Jolie…"

"Shh. Don't say anything." She moved toward the bed with a quiet, unstudied grace that surprised her. Here she was, involved in the most important moment of her life, and she didn't feel the least uncertainty, the least inhibited. She was a woman prepared, a smart woman with built-in protection for once-in-a-lifetime moments such as this.

He wrapped his arms around her waist and buried his face in the soft contours of her belly. Weaving her fingers through his hair, she leaned into him, crooning. Not words, really, but a heart song that released courage and comfort. For him. For her. For the two of them together.

They stayed that way for a small eternity, his breath warm on her skin and her heart beating desperately against her rib cage. Jolie didn't dare breathe for fear this wonder would vanish. Tight with tension, edgy with passion, she forced herself to patience, willed herself to a stillness that accepted whatever would come.

She felt the change in him, the unleashing of a force so powerful that she was borne backward toward the bed, down to the sheets, where he hovered over her like a dark angel. Holding her captive with a piercing stare, he stripped aside his clothes and tossed them on the floor.

He was wonderfully and gloriously made—his chest sculpted and smooth, his belly lean and hard, his legs fine and powerful. Under normal circumstances she might have said, "You are amazing," but these were not ordinary circumstances. Lancelot was no ordinary man.

He was a phoenix risen from the ashes of a guarded and secret place. He was a ticking bomb set to explode, and God help her, she didn't want it to happen until she knew the pleasures of his flesh joined with hers.

Call her selfish. Call her practical. But she remained silent against the pillows, watching and waiting.

She felt the heat of his burning eyes all the way to her bones. A deep shudder shook him, and he closed his eyes.

Oh, please don't let him change his mind.

Without a word he parted her thighs and slid deep inside. Suddenly, there was paradise. She wanted to sing. She wanted to shout. But most of all she wanted to keep holding the silent, intense man who made love to her as if there were no tomorrow.

They were tireless together, insatiable. As the rain beat against the window they created magic time and

again, giving and receiving in a deep silence that was
almost spiritual.

I love you, I love you.

The words played continuously through her mind,
but she kept her secret. This was not the right time
for revelations of the heart.

Would there ever be a time?

Jolie didn't know. All she knew was that she
would take whatever Lance offered, because not to
have him at all would be unthinkable.

Chapter Seventeen

Lance blocked everything out of his mind except the moment and the woman who flowed beneath him like a river. He rode the amazing currents, drowned in them, emerged reborn, only to drown again.

Never had he known a woman like Jolie. Never had he allowed a woman to touch his heart, his soul. Never had he loved. He loved her and he needed her. It was that simple, that scary.

His need and her passion drove him to his limits and beyond. Somehow he found the strength and the stamina of an eighteen-year-old.

It was almost dawn by the time he left her bed. Too full to speak, he brushed her damp hair back from her face, kissed her softly on the lips, then went through the connecting door without a word.

What was there to say? "I can't make promises" said it all. Beyond that he could only complicate matters more.

Lance fell into his bed too tired to think. Grateful for that small respite from his conscience, he slept deeply for five hours.

When he woke up he padded to the window still naked, and saw water dripping from the eaves. The capricious Mississippi weather had warmed enough to start a meltdown of the ice it had dumped across the unsuspecting land the night before.

He went to the connecting door, but didn't hear any signs of movement from Jolie's side. Let her sleep. The roads were passable now, but there was no hurry.

He called Elizabeth on his cell phone to tell her they would be late getting to O'Banyon Manor.

"Where are you, Lance?"

He told her, giving only the bare essentials and leaving out the most important parts.

"You really care for Kat, don't you, Lance?"

More than you'll ever know.

"She's a fine woman, Elizabeth. You're lucky to have her for a sister."

"I know. Listen, I have plenty of preproduction chores to do, and several other interviews I can slide into your slot. Take your time over there. Two or three days if you like.''

One more night like last night and he would never leave Jolie's side.

''The weather's clearing. We'll be home tonight,'' he told her, and she agreed.

Thank God she didn't second-guess him and dish out advice. He felt privileged to count her as his friend.

After he'd hung up, he listened at the door once more. Hearing only echoing silence, he lay down, not to sleep but merely to rest his eyes.

There was a certain way a woman felt after being thoroughly loved—languorous and full of delicious secrets, satisfied to the bone and yet eager for the touch that would drive her wild again.

Smiling, Jolie pulled the covers up to her chin and hummed. Not a tune, really. Merely several happy notes strung together in a breathy sort of way.

It was still gray and gloomy outside. Water ran down the windowpane, which meant the temperature was rising. But if weather patterns held, it would be afternoon before the roads cleared completely.

Jolie glanced at the connecting door. Would Lance come through?

Probably not. Last night would never have happened if she hadn't been bold. Somehow she'd found a crack in the fortress that surrounded him, but that didn't mean the walls had come tumbling down. He was probably on the other side of the door shoring up his weak spots.

Jolie punched her pillow and tried to go back to sleep, but she was too wound up. She could put on her clothes and get breakfast at the motel's modest food bar, but she didn't really want food. She wanted Lance.

This was her last chance.

The truth blazed across her mind, and she shoved back the covers. After today there would be no more chance meetings and gift-from-the-gods icy roads. Once she and Lance were back at O'Banyon Manor, he would keep out of her path. Then, after Elizabeth finished filming, Jolie might never see him again.

So, what did she have to lose?

She didn't even bother with clothes; she simply eased the door open, then slipped into the darkened room where he lay sleeping, the curtains drawn and the covers kicked back.

Jolie climbed in beside him and pulled the sheet around his chilled body. He came instantly awake.

"Jolie?"

"Shh. Let me." She slid under the sheet, and whatever resistance she felt in him vanished immediately. He hauled her up and made love to her with the same silent intensity he'd used the night before.

She longed for him to speak. She longed to hear

I love you, I adore you, you are precious to me, I want to spend the rest of my life with you.

Pipe dreams. She might as well wish for the moon. And yet....

His breath fanned warm across her cheek and in unguarded moments he buried his face in her hair and whispered her name. The way he said it was like a prayer, a song, a promise.

But he'd said there would be no promises. Jolie had entered into this overnight affair with her eyes wide-open. When she left his bed she would not be the same woman. She would never be the same again. But neither would she be disillusioned.

There was always hope, wasn't there?

When they finally fell across the bed, sated, their skin warm to the touch, sweat dripping off their bodies in spite of the chill outside, Jolie lifted herself on her elbows.

"I understand what you told me last night, Lance, and I want you to know I'm okay with it." She got off the bed, gathered the sheet around her, toga-style, then stood looking down at him, wishing for what she couldn't have.

"Someday, somewhere my prince will come and carry me off to live happily ever after. If the Fates are kind, it will be you."

She kissed him softly on the lips, then went through the connecting door and leaned against it, trying not to cry.

Be brave, she told herself, but it was hard to be brave when you were wearing nothing but a bedsheet and beard burns. It was hard to be brave when your heart was breaking in two.

Jolie was quiet on the drive back to the nursing home to get Lance's motorcycle. He glanced over at her and said, "Are you okay?" and when she said she was, he felt relief that labeled him a coward. Or worse.

Last night he'd broken all his own rules. After vowing to himself that he would never sleep with this woman without promises, what had he done? Spent the entire night reveling in her arms. As if that weren't bad enough, he'd let his guard down again this morning. Heck, he hadn't even put up a token resistance.

It wouldn't happen again. He'd make sure of that.

Mercifully, the drive to Hanging Grapes Haven was short. He parked beside his bike, and Jolie slid over to take the wheel.

Leaning in at the open door, he said, "You be careful now."

"I will."

She looked at him with soft, luminous eyes that made him feel both heroic and cowardly. God, he was so confused he didn't know which way was up.

He lingered beside her car, but there was nothing else to say, so he closed her door and walked away without looking back. He fiddled around with his bike till he heard her turn around and head out of the parking lot. Then he followed, closely enough to see that she didn't get into any trouble, but far enough back so that he couldn't make out her face in the rearview mirror.

There was only so much temptation a man could stand.

Elizabeth greeted them at the front door, and immediately immersed them in her high energy and lofty plans.

"I'm so glad to see you. What perfect timing. Lance, I'd like to film you first, if you don't mind."

"Just give me a chance to change." He rubbed his chin. "And shave."

"Great. You know the way to your room."

Oh, God. Connecting doors. Again.

"I do. Give me twenty minutes."

Elizabeth laughed. "Thirty, tops."

Lance looked Jolie's way and fell briefly into her eyes, then tore himself away and raced upstairs. The first thing he did when he got inside his bedroom was draw the bolt on the connecting door.

It wouldn't stop him, of course, but if insanity overtook him in the middle of the night it might slow him down enough for him to come to his senses.

Elizabeth had set up her cameras in the library, the camera crew was nowhere in sight. But more importantly, neither was Jolie.

"The crew went for a barbecue, and Kat's with Mom. They went to Ben's house to help pick out the furniture she wants to move over here when they merge households," Elizabeth told him.

"Was I that obvious?"

"Yes. Look, Lance, you don't have to pretend with me."

"I know that. You've proved yourself a good friend."

"I want to show you something." She went to the bookshelves and returned with a dog-eared book of fairy tales. Flipping it open, she came to a color picture of a woman in medieval costume being carried off on a white stallion by a man wearing a crown. The faded stain on the page looked suspiciously like chocolate.

"Sleeping Beauty and her prince. Kat got this book for Christmas when she was four years old. This is her favorite story. I can't tell you how many times she made me or Matt read it to her."

"While she ate chocolate?"

"How did you know?"

"I know *her*."

"Well, then you don't need me to tell you this. Matt always thought she loved this story best because of the picture of the white horse, but I think she loved it best because deep down Kat is a true blue romantic."

Elizabeth closed the book and put it back on the

shelf. "If you ever decide you're interested, Kat needs real romance."

"You're a good woman."

"And you're a good man." Elizabeth studied him. "Are you comfortable now? Warmed up? Ready to start filming?"

Smiling, he nodded. "I take back what I said about *good*. You're a *devious* woman, Elizabeth Coltrane."

"Don't tell." She handed him a typewritten sheet of paper. "Take a look at these questions. Basically, I'm going to ask how you met the woman called Birdie, under what circumstances, and what has transpired since. Just tell the truth."

"Including the part about her stealing the O'Banyon family's Christmas?"

"Especially that. It's colorful, and a great human interest angle." The crew came into the library just then, and for the next few minutes Elizabeth was busy giving instructions.

Finally she said, "Okay, everybody. Places. Let's get started."

All the way back from Ben's house, Lucy talked about weddings. Not that Jolie minded weddings. On the contrary, she was always the one who grabbed the June brides' section of the newspaper every summer when they featured local debs modeling their chosen finery. Lucy had paid little attention, and Elizabeth none at all.

Now here was Lucy, chatting about a wedding as she drove hill and dale. And here was her youngest daughter, who ought to be happy, taking exception because she wasn't the bride-to-be. How tacky could you get?

Thank goodness it was too dark for her mother to see her expression.

Lucy twisted around to face her abruptly. "I'm thinking about wearing purple. What do you think?"

Jolie grabbed for the wheel and steered the car away from the shoulder. "I think you're not going to live to be a bride if you don't watch the road."

"Sorry. Of course, Elizabeth will want me to wear white.... Well, I guess she will. With her you never know."

"White. She's a romantic at heart."

"I never noticed that. How do you know?

"Because she used to read "Sleeping Beauty" to me all the time. She loved that story."

"Hmm. Michael hasn't called since she got here. I wonder what's going on?"

"Oh, you know Elizabeth. When she works, she *works*."

"She works too hard, if you ask me. She ought to read my latest book. She might learn a thing or two."

"I certainly did."

Lucy laughed. "Good. Beats having to give those dreadful birds-and-bees talks to my children."

"Mom, I'm hardly a child."

"Just kidding. You know, of course, I'll want you to be a bridesmaid."

"Great." She'd have to buy a bridesmaid dress and dye a pair of satin shoes a color nobody would be caught dead in.

Jolie was glad when the ride was finally over, and even happier when she discovered that everybody else had gone to bed. She wouldn't have to stand around and pretend.

The only painful part of this visit with her family was that everybody expected her to be cheerful. Nobody expected it of Elizabeth. She was the studious, serious type.

And then there was Jolie. All she needed was a bulb nose, red rag hair and some big clown shoes.

Jolie kissed her mother good-night, then went upstairs and stood in the middle of her bedroom staring at the connecting door.

"Open sesame," she whispered, but of course, it didn't.

And she wasn't about to go through.

She put on a nightshirt that said Save the Rain Forests, then went to bed determined to sleep. After she'd counted two hundred and fifty-nine sheep, she gave up, went to her closet and rummaged around on the top shelf till she found her old childhood pal, a raggedy lion.

"Hello, Beast. Long time no see."

She lay down with the stuffed toy cuddled under

her arm, then started giggling, thinking what a good story this would make for Connie.

What did you do last night, Jolie?

I went to bed with a beast.

Connie would laugh, and so would Jolie.

There wasn't enough laughter in this world.

She'd always known that truth in her bones.

And maybe that's why she wouldn't strike clown off her list in her attempts at self-improvement.

Lance stood at the bolted door, arguing with his conscience.

Lift the latch. You've already made love with her. What difference does it make now?

Because he loved her, damn it. If he went through the door now, it would be a commitment of sorts, and he was far from ready for that.

Jolie needed declarations of love. She needed a wedding in a big church, with all her family in attendance. She needed romance. Hadn't Elizabeth told him that?

Lance leaned his head against the door and breathed deeply. He ached so much for her he could barely move. He caught a whiff of her fragrance. Or was it his imagination?

When he got his passion under control, he put his hand on the door and whispered, ''Good night, my love.'' Then he climbed into his cold, lonely bed.

Chapter Eighteen

Goodbyes were never easy, especially saying goodbye to Jolie.

He said his farewells to Elizabeth and her mother
first. Then finally to the one who mattered most.

"Jolie." She turned toward him with a wistful
look that caught him high under the breastbone and
wouldn't let go. "I just came to say goodbye."

"You're leaving? So soon?"

"Elizabeth's finished with me, and I've received
an assignment in Richmond, Virginia. I have to be
there tomorrow."

Jolie shot him a brave smile that nearly broke his
heart. "Well, then, take care." The small hand she

offered was a shocking reminder of how explosive contact with her could be.

"You, too."

"I will always remember you, Lancelot."

He didn't want to raise false hopes, so he kept the truth to himself. He would never forget *her*. How could he? She was the only woman who had ever made him feel completely comfortable in his own skin, the only woman who had ever made him wish for a home to call his own.

Still, he couldn't say those things. Not yet. "Don't go chasing after any more thieves," he finally said.

"Not without my mop and soccer pads."

God, that smile. He had to get out before he did something foolish. Still, he couldn't walk away from that smile, that sweet upturned face that moved him most when it had a little chocolate smear near the mouth. A mouth he had kissed. A mouth he was going to kiss again. Audience or no audience.

He cupped her face, then kissed her tenderly on the lips, a small, brief kiss that made his heart beg for more. Wisely, he ignored his inner pleadings.

"Goodbye, Jolie," he whispered, and then he left quickly, without looking back.

By the time Jolie finished her part in Elizabeth's documentary, her face was frozen into a permanent mask of false merriment. She'd have to use a crowbar to pry her mouth back into its natural shape.

Two days after Lance had left, Jolie headed back to Memphis. She had been home no more than fifteen minutes when Connie came over to discuss her wedding plans.

Her neighbor prefaced her monologue with "I've just got a minute, I'm on my lunch break," and ended with, "You'll be my bridesmaid, of course."

That meant more dyed-to-match shoes. By the time Jolie finished being a bridesmaid for all those weddings, she'd have enough tacky satin shoes in Easter egg colors to open her own shoe store. On the bright side, if her job with the SPCA didn't come through she'd have another way to shore up her income.

"I'll be happy to," she told Connie.

"You don't look happy. What's wrong?"

Jolie wasn't about to reveal intimate details. Not even to her best friend. Some things simply weren't meant for sharing, and what she'd felt during those beautiful hours in Lancelot's arms fell into that category.

"It was lovely while it lasted, and then he said goodbye. I knew he would because he told me he couldn't make promises."

"Don't worry about it. They all say that at first. If it's meant to be, he'll come around."

"You're talking *fate* here. Do you believe in that stuff?"

"Yeah. Tarot cards and auras and numerology,

too. You never know. The world is full of mysteries.''

''Yeah, like why hasn't the SPCA called about my job application? Do you think I forgot to put my phone number on the form?''

''I don't know. You might try calling them.''

But as Connie was getting ready to leave, the phone rang. Jolie answered, then stood there speechless while her friend mouthed, *Are you all right?*

She hung up, then stood paralyzed with shock. Connie grabbed her shoulders.

''Kat, say something.''

''I got the job.''

''Let's go somewhere and celebrate.''

''We'll celebrate here. I'll cook.''

''You can't cook.''

''Lance taught me.''

He had taught her many things, among them, how to feel like a woman well loved. But she wouldn't dwell on that now. She had a great new job, and dinner to cook.

Her new workspace in downtown Memphis couldn't actually be classified as an office, but Jolie referred to it as one, anyway. Giving the cubicle an important label made her feel as if she had accomplished one of her major goals: moving up the career ladder. Shoot, she was barely on the first rung, but she would be working three days a week doing publicity for the SPCA, which meant, even with cutting back her pet grooming to two days, she'd still come out ahead. And if she did a good job at the SPCA, she would move up the ladder.

With her increased income she'd be able to afford lovely surprises for Birdie. Shoot, she could even get a few things for herself—maybe that pasta machine recommended by some of the world's best gourmet cooks. With practice, she could cook holiday feasts for her family without Lance's help.

Oh, help.

She traced the design on the tooled leather desk set he'd given her. It looked wonderful. And important. Like Jolie was going to be *somebody.*

Well, heck, she already was. Just ask Jimmy Stewart.

Jolie glanced around her tiny space to see if she had room for Jimmy, but decided she didn't. Besides, she needed to make a good impression, and talking to a cardboard man might not be the best way to do that.

It had been two weeks since he'd last seen Jolie, and Lance was surviving. But not living. He maintained a molelike existence, buried in his work by day and in his search for family by night. All clues led right back to Phoenix. Still, there had been no word from Clyde Shane, so another trip would be useless. Clyde was not the kind of man who caved under pressure.

Leaving his computer screen glowing, Lance stood at the window looking at the surrounding houses. He would be in Richmond only for the duration of this assignment, so he was in another borrowed neighborhood. It shouldn't matter to him what the houses looked like or who lived in them, since he would be there such a short time, but it did. The houses were old and rich with history. Judging from the large number of senior citizens and children, they were filled with extended families.

He could see Jolie in a neighborhood like this. He could picture her inviting her parents and her husband's parents to live with her when they could no longer take care of themselves. He imagined her humming through spacious rooms while children played on the swing set in the backyard and two sets of grandparents, and aunts and uncles, gathered in the living room for another holiday feast.

She deserved that.

He jerked the curtain shut as if he could shut out his thoughts, as well as the neighborhood. The computer screen blinked at him from his desk.

He cut the power. What was the use? He was too disheartened to continue the search for family. He'd already said goodbye to Jolie. He'd said he could make no promises.

So let it go. Get on with your life.

He flipped on the television and was surfing aimlessly through the channels when his cell phone rang. It was Clyde Shane, and he was ready to talk.

Clyde and his wife, Lydia, flew to Richmond the next day. She was a pretty woman, small and dark. The photograph Lance has seen on her husband's desk didn't do her justice, probably because it was hard to capture a lively spirit on film.

They came to his house at nine o'clock in the evening, bearing photograph albums and a leather-bound diary with an eagle embossed on the cover. Sitting in the straight-backed chairs in the apartment's combination dining and living room, Clyde spread the items on the table.

"My wife made me come," he said. "If it hadn't been for Lydia, I would still be in Phoenix."

"No, you wouldn't, Clyde." She patted his hand. "You'd have come around to the right way eventually."

Lance itched to see inside the albums, to thumb through the diary. To hear the words he'd waited for all his life: *I know who you are.* Trained for discipline and patience, he waited.

Clyde's hand shook when he opened the first album to a photograph of a young girl with big dark eyes and familiar cheekbones.

"This is Sarah," he said. "My sister, your mother."

Lance had dreamed this moment a thousand times. He'd dreamed what he would do—laugh, cry, shout. He did none of those things. Instead he looked into the eyes of the man who had just become family and said, "Thank you."

Clyde reached out and Lance clasped his hand, while Lydia rummaged around in her purse for her handkerchief.

"I told Clyde you're the only thing we have left of Sarah, and that she'd want us to make you a part of our lives. If you'll have us, we'd like to be family to you."

"I'd like that. Very much." Lance studied the picture of his mother. She was so young, hardly more than a child herself. "I'd like to hear her story."

"There were six of us children," Clyde said. "Daddy had been killed in a construction accident when I was five years old. In order to keep the family together, Mother did every kind of odd job she could—washing, baby-sitting, baking."

"That's why Sarah...my mother...." The words clogged in Lance's throat and he had to clear it before he could finish his question. "That's why she was selling cookies?"

"Yes. We were doing okay till Sarah got leukemia."

"Is that how she died?"

"Yes. And that's why she left you at the orphanage. She knew she was going to die, and she knew

Mother couldn't take on any more responsibility. The medical bills had strained her almost to the breaking point.''

''Do you know who my father was?''

''No. Sarah never told us, and we didn't try to find out. She was never wild, hardly dated, even. I think she wanted so desperately to live that she grabbed hold of the first boy who made her feel as if life would go on forever.''

''I've never hated my mother for giving me away.''

''I'm glad. I know this doesn't make up to you for all those years alone, but she grieved for you till the day she died.''

''I don't live in the past, and I don't assign blame. All I wanted was to know my name.''

''Shane is a good name. A name you can be proud of. And we'd be proud for you to take it.''

Lance didn't know how he felt about that right now. He'd wanted to know, that was all. He'd never gone beyond the moment of discovering the truth.

''I don't say that lightly,'' Clyde added. ''I did some research, too. You're a brave and honorable man, no matter what the press has said. You're not afraid to put your life on the line for your country. Apache blood runs strong and true in you.''

The burden of guilt Lance had carried since his partner's death suddenly lifted. Clyde gave him more than the gift of family; he gave him the gift of vindication and affirmation.

"Thank you."

Lydia put her hand over his. "Please do give serious thought to taking the name Shane. It belongs to you."

"I'll think about it," he said.

They spent the rest of the evening looking at family albums that spanned Sarah's short life, with Clyde and Lydia telling Lance stories to go with the pictures.

Overloaded with emotion, he watched Clyde turn the last page, then close the album. Lance felt a sense of completeness and yet strangely empty. His mother's history filled the empty spaces in him, expanded into every sinew and bone until there was no room for the negatives—unworthy, nameless, lonely.

Clyde handed him an envelope containing copies of the photographs seen in the albums, as well as a worn, leather-bound diary.

"This is yours. I never read it, never wanted to intrude on Sarah's privacy, even after all these years."

After they had gone Lance locked the diary in his desk. He would read it someday. Right now he was too raw. He had too much to think about. For one thing, he needed to figure out just what role a family named Shane would play in his life. For another, he needed to think about his name.

But most of all, he needed to think about a woman who had breezed into his life wearing soccer pads and a baseball cap, then breezed out holding a cardboard cutout of Jimmy Stewart, and Lancelot's heart.

Chapter Nineteen

Jolie couldn't wait to get home. Her first day on her new job was over—*finally*—and all she wanted to do was lie down on the sofa with a heating pad on her cold feet and a big cup of hot chocolate with lots of whipped cream on top within easy reach.

Not that she hadn't liked her job. On the contrary, she loved it. It was the computer she hated. More precisely, the computer program. Give her a dog brush and a pair of sharp precision scissors and she could shine like a quasar. But put her in charge of a computer whose programs had obviously been written in secret code by Chinese stand-up comics, and she was lost.

She'd felt as if she'd been abandoned in the Sahara Desert without water and a map, let alone a compass. It was a conspiracy between the Chinese and Marsha Hughes, her terminally cheerful supervisor. She'd spent all of ten minutes instructing Jolie in the finer points of her job, then she'd trotted off to the coffee machine saying breezily, "Don't worry about a thing. You'll be just great."

Maybe sometime in the next century. Meanwhile, Jolie merely wanted to be sane and unconfused.

She'd finally gotten back to her apartment, fixed her chocolate and was just stretching out when the phone rang. Wouldn't you know it? She thought about letting it ring. It was probably Connie wondering how her day had gone. Or Elizabeth, or her mother.

"Go away." Jolie glared at her telephone, but it kept on ringing. She dragged herself off the sofa. "Hello."

"Jolie? Is everything okay?"

"Lance. Oh, Lord, *Lance.* Is that you?"

"It is. How are you?"

"Oh, my gosh… I'm sorry I was so surly."

His laughter thrilled her all the way to her toes. "You? Surly? You couldn't be surly if you tried."

Was he flirting with her? That's what it felt like. Furthermore, he sounded so lighthearted she could hardly believe he was the same man.

"Where are you?" she asked.

"Richmond...Jolie, are you crying?"

"Yes."

"You don't have any tissue, do you?"

She glanced around the room. Naturally, the tissue box was empty and had been since last Tuesday. She'd meant to put it on her list of things to buy, but in all the excitement over her new job, she forgot.

"No."

"I'll hang on while you go blow your nose. Don't worry. I'm not going anywhere."

She raced to the bathroom, blew her nose, then pulled off a length of toilet paper and carried it back to the den, just in case. From the way things were shaping up, this could turn out to be a six-hankie phone call.

"Hi, I'm back." She settled comfortably in a corner of the sofa, then propped her feet on the coffee table with the cooling chocolate.

He didn't answer, and for a while Jolie thought the phone connection had gone dead. Finally, he said, "Jolie, I've found my family."

She listened while he told her about his upbringing in the orphanage, his search for his mother and finally the visit from his uncle, Clyde Shane. Jolie went through every bit of her toilet tissue and wished she had more.

"I'm filing a motion to add Shane as my middle name," he said finally.

"Lance Shane Estes." She tried the name out to

see how it would sound, and it sounded wonderful. If she'd had a piece of paper she'd have written *Mrs. Lance Shane Estes* twenty-five times. "That's such a beautiful story I could cry."

"You *are* crying." The way he said it felt like a hug. She hung on to the phone, savoring the idea. "I wish I were there to hold you."

"You do?"

"Yes. Jolie, I'd like to see you again, if you'll let me."

Let him? Good Lord, she'd get down on her knees and *beg* him. She was just on the verge of admitting as much when she recalled how Connie had told her that men loved the chase.

Well, she wasn't going to deprive him of the pleasure of pursuit. But neither was she going to play hard to get. She didn't believe in playing games.

"I'd like that."

"There's something you have to know first. My job is extremely dangerous, and I'm gone a lot. If that matters to you, I need to know now."

She was going to die of happiness on the spot. Good gracious, he was *serious.* And he deserved a real answer, not a quick response that she might later regret.

"I don't think it matters, Lance, but it would be less than fair of me to say no, then change my mind."

''Think about it, Jolie. Take all the time you need. You can call me and let me know.''

She wrote down the number he gave her, then he said goodbye. The minute she hung up the phone she panicked. What if he changed his mind? What if he decided she wasn't worth the trouble? What if he met some gorgeous woman who had far more to offer than she, and fell instantly in love and didn't care whether he ever heard from Jolie Kat Coltrane again?

Jolie jerked up the receiver and started punching in his number. Halfway through she put it back down. He'd think she was an idiot.

She needed time to think. She needed advice.

She called Connie.

Lance hadn't expected a quick and easy agreement from Jolie, had he? What was it Elizabeth had said? She's a romantic.

Okay, so Jolie hadn't said, Of course your work doesn't matter, come straight up to Memphis and sweep me off my feet and into your bed. But that didn't mean he had to sit around staring at the telephone, hoping. Once Lance made up his mind about a thing, he didn't dally; he took action.

Full of purpose, he got the phone book, looked in the yellow pages till he found what he wanted, then made his call. He was a man with a plan.

Connie came over bearing sour cream and onion dip, and Jolie provided potato chips. They were sitting with their feet propped up on Jolie's coffee table, eating their way through Jolie's problem, which Connie insisted wasn't a problem at all.

"Look, Kat, from what you've told me, you're crazy about this man. Am I right?"

"Right. But what if something awful did happen to him? I'd absolutely *die*."

"So you want to spend the rest of your life by yourself, or maybe with the wrong man, simply because you're scared of losing him?"

"I wouldn't put it that way."

"How would you put it?"

"I'm being sensible, that's all."

Connie snorted. "You should be sensible about jobs and walking shoes and winter coats. Not about the man of your heart. Good grief, Kat."

The doorbell rang, and Connie fueled herself with chips and dip while Jolie answered the door. It was a delivery boy with a dozen yellow roses.

"These are for *me?*"

"They are if you're Jolie Kat Coltrane." She nodded. "Sign here, please."

Connie screamed when she saw the roses. "Open the card," she yelled. "Hurry up, I want to know what it says."

"It says, 'For my favorite girl in soccer pads, Lance.' I think I'm going to cry."

Connie went to the bathroom and came back with

a wad of toilet tissue. "Here. Use this. Let me see that card. He calls you his 'favorite girl.' He's serious, Kat."

"You think so?"

"Listen, do you know what a dozen long-stemmed roses cost? Men who aren't serious don't send flowers. Trust me."

"Does Wayne send flowers to you?"

"Yeah, but only on special occasions. You know, birthdays and Valentine's. Do you think I should give back the ring?"

"You're *serious?*"

"Heck, no. I'm just kidding. Still...these are pure heaven."

Jolie buried her face in the soft, fragrant petals and inhaled. *Roses.* No one had ever sent her roses.

Connie came over and squeezed Jolie's shoulder. "I could get hit by a cab crossing the street. Nothing's ever certain. It's up to you whether you want to play it safe or take the risk."

Lance used his harmonica to relieve stress. Since his call to Jolie, he'd been sitting in his apartment playing one sad song after another, many of them from the World War II era: "Saturday Night Is the Loneliest Night of the Week," "I'll Walk Alone," "I'll Be Seeing You," "Ev'ry Time We Say Goodbye."

Not many people his age had even heard of those

songs, let alone appreciated them. Danny had, which was one of the reasons he and Lance had been perfectly suited as partners.

Lance's new partner, John Braden, was a nice enough guy, but he didn't know blues from Adam's house cat. He couldn't hold a candle to Danny. John had called shortly after Lance talked to Jolie, and invited him out for a few beers. "Just to unwind," he'd said, but Lance wasn't ready yet to become chummy. Maybe he never would. He didn't know. All he knew was that he needed to be by himself playing sad music this evening. Somehow it made the waiting easier.

He was in the midst of "Time on My Hands" when his phone rang.

"Lance, it's Jolie."

Chapter Twenty

One week after Jolie's call, Lance was on a plane to Memphis for dinner and a weekend. "To see how it goes," she had said.

At least she hadn't said no. To tell the truth, her cautionary note fit well with his plans, too. Love was unfamiliar territory to him. Furthermore, it was serious territory, and he didn't want to make any mistakes.

Without the distractions of family and holidays and Birdie, he and Jolie would get a chance to see if what they felt was real. She was making dinner. That would be great. A nice quiet evening in her apartment with lots of time to talk.

Tomorrow, he'd take her to the movies, maybe a walk along the river if it wasn't too cold, then to the historic Peabody Hotel for dinner. He'd done his research. It was a landmark in the heart of downtown Memphis with ducks that paraded down a red carpet to the ornate fountain in the lobby.

There was lots to see in Memphis. The Peabody was only a few blocks from Sun Studios, where some of the early rock and roll stars had cut records. They could even tour Graceland, home of The King. Lance loved Elvis's music. He sometimes played it on his harmonica when the mood struck.

He'd brought his blues harp. Maybe they'd have time to sit around and play and sing. He'd get a chance to make certain Jolie was the kind of woman who knew the art of simple pleasures. He'd find out if what he remembered from the holidays—that she was a lively woman who required no fancy trappings or exotic entertainment to be happy—was real and lasting.

And of course, he'd sleep on the sofa. Clearly, she was a passionate woman. No question about that, and no need to cloud the rest of the issues with sex. His memories were vivid. Without a doubt she was his perfect mate in that arena.

His excitement built with every minute that brought him closer to Jolie. By the time his plane touched down in Memphis, he was perspiring with excitement, though the temperature was in the mid-

thirties and a weatherman on Channel 3 predicted a
further drop.

Lance hurried to the baggage claim, past travelers
bundled in boots and coats. He didn't care about the
weather. He had other things on his mind, namely
getting his bag and grabbing a cab.

Just when he thought his bag had been sent on a
sightseeing trip to Houston, Texas by way of Port-
land, Oregon, the carousel coughed up his suitcase.
He grabbed it and didn't have any trouble hailing a
cab. There were some advantages to being a tall man
with a face like a hatchet. Most people didn't mess
with Lancelot Estes.

Soon to be Lancelot Shane Estes. He'd filed the
papers on Monday.

As the cab hurtled through the darkness, Lance
leaned over and asked the driver, "How much far-
ther?"

"Ten minutes."

It felt like ten hours.

Jolie checked her stuffed chicken for the tenth
time. It was roasting perfectly. The oven timer was
set, so she didn't have to worry about overcooking.
The bean casserole was made and sitting in the
warmer. She'd wait until they'd had drinks to put on
the rice and make the salad. No need to rush right
into dinner. Let him unwind, get over his travel fa-
tigue. That way they'd have a chance to talk. She

could find out if memory had elevated him to heroic proportions or if he really was the prince of her dreams.

She hurried to the bathroom to check her hair and spritz herself with perfume, then raced back to the kitchen for one more peek at the chicken. *Perfect.*

When the doorbell rang she nearly jumped out of her skin. *Okay, be calm. Say hello, then offer him a drink. Pour the wine. Listen to music.*

The music... Lord, she'd forgotten the music. The doorbell pinged again.

"Coming." On the way to the door, she flipped on the CD player. Eric Clapton's "Wonderful To-night" filled the room.

She swung open the door, and there Lance was, every bit as gorgeous and wonderful as she remembered.

"Hello," she said, feeling suddenly shy.

"Hello again." He handed her a box of Godiva chocolates and a bottle of Italian wine. "These are for you."

"Oh, I *love* chocolates."

"I know."

Her hand touched his when she accepted the gifts, and that was all it took. Putting them on the table beside the door, she went straight into his arms. Bending to her, he kissed her as if he was returning from war. She melted against him, then backed into the room.

A sane part of her mind said, *Okay, a greeting kiss is fine. To be expected, really, considering what we had in Pontotoc. After the kiss, we'll talk.*

Eric Clapton finished ''Wonderful Tonight'' and moved into ''Ain't That Lovin' You'' before they came up for air.

''I've missed you,'' Lance whispered against her hair. ''More than you'll ever know.''

''I've missed you, too.''

Jolie's heart was pounding so hard she could barely breathe. Looking deep into his eyes, she was sucked back into a maelstrom of emotions. Suddenly, they were kissing again, kissing with an urgency and a mounting passion that demanded release.

The bedroom was only a few feet away, the door standing open. They walked that way, locked together and stepped, still kissing, until she felt the backs of her knees pressed against the bed.

They fumbled with buttons, zippers, snaps. With their clothes in a heap they tumbled onto Jolie's fluffy quilted comforter and came together as naturally as if they'd been born for each other.

And suddenly Jolie knew heaven. He was everything she remembered, and more, for this time Lance was no silent lover.

He murmured his wonder and appreciation with each new discovery. As he explored her body from head to toe, he whispered, ''You are so beautiful. I love your belly button, your knees, your toes.''

She sizzled, she sighed and she giggled. Making love with Lance was fun. What a discovery! To have all that passion, all that intensity, and laughter, too.

She found a little scar on his belly. "What is this?"

"Knife fight."

She kissed it, then said, "There, now, I've made it all better."

"Yes...yes, you have."

He kissed her mouth, her nose, her ear, the freckles on her shoulder. "I love these," he said, then kissed them again and moved back to her lips.

Then they were beyond talking, beyond exploring. With her face in his shoulder and her body moving silently to his rhythm, Jolie thought, *This is all I need to know. This love that makes everything else insignificant by comparison.*

In a world full of uncertainty, Jolie was blessed to have one sure thing—a love strong enough for whatever came next, a love that would endure, no matter what.

Around midnight Lance said, "Is that chicken I smell?"

"Yes. Stuffed with mushrooms and onions."

"My sweet little gourmet." He kissed her nose. "I'm hungry."

They dashed into the kitchen, naked and laughing, then ate a very late dinner of chicken and beans, sitting side by side and reaching out every now and then to touch.

"I was going to cook rice and make a salad," she said.

"That's okay. I know a better way to spend that time."

"So do I." With a mischievous grin, she led him back to bed.

Jolie woke up to the delicious smells of cooking. Grabbing her robe, she hurried into her kitchen, and there was Lance in jeans and a too-small apron, preparing a feast.

"Good morning, sleepyhead." Smiling, he folded her in his arms and kissed her.

I would walk to the ends of the earth for his smile. And this wonderful feeling of being held safe from all harm.

She smiled back. "Hey, handsome. I was going to fix breakfast in bed for you." She glanced at the clock. "Well, brunch."

"That's what I'm doing for you." He kissed her again. "Now, hurry back to bed and when I come with a breakfast feast, pretend you're surprised and amazed."

"I am. I am completely amazed that you're here in my apartment, in my kitchen."

"I'm here…loving you. I love you, Jolie."

"Oh! Oh my gosh. You love me? You really do?"

"Yes, I love you. I really do."

She launched herself at him and he held her close, kissing her, tears and all. Then pulled a handkerchief from his pocket, and she cried freely, not worrying about mascara.

She loved kitchens. She was going to order two bronze plaques and put one where they now stood, the other in the kitchen at O'Banyon Manor, where they'd first met.

Lance kissed her again, and breakfast in bed had to wait a while.

Jolie's weekend with Lance ended all too quickly, and before she knew it she was in the car taking him to the airport.

"I'm already missing you."

"I'll call every night." He handed her his handkerchief, then kissed her, grabbed his bag and vanished inside the terminal.

She probably would have sat there another fifteen minutes if the security guard hadn't motioned her on. She couldn't cry and drive in heavy traffic, so she stopped crying. When she got to a residential section where traffic would be light, she'd resume.

But Elizabeth foiled that plan. She called on Jolie's cell phone to talk about Michael.

"Guess what? He called."

"That's a good thing, isn't it?"

"I'm not speaking to him, and he knows it."

"Maybe if you saw him, you two could patch things up."

"Hell will freeze over before I see him."

"Well, if you feel that way…"

"I most certainly do. Hey, you sound stopped up. Are you getting a cold?"

"Probably. They're still predicting snow up here."

"What does snow have to do with anything?"

"You know, everybody staying inside and spreading germs."

Jolie felt a small twinge of guilt. After all, Elizabeth had confided in her about Michael. Still, what was there to say? Lance had said *I love you,* but that didn't translate into wedding bells.

"By the way, Elizabeth, I have a new job." She went into great detail describing her office and her work, and by the time she'd finished, even she thought she'd landed a really important position. And it was. Saving animals was a noble cause.

"That's great, Jolie. I'm proud of you."

"And I'm taking a night course at Memphis State. Spanish." When Elizabeth laughed, Jolie said, "I know, I know. You were right. I'm going to see if I can enroll in a computer course, too. I need to make friends with Godzilla."

"Who's Godzilla?"

"The computer at my office."

By the time Jolie finished her conversation and got home, she was out of the crying mood. Which was a good thing, because Connie was waiting for her on the top step of the staircase outside her apartment.

The first thing her friend said was, "Since when did you start wearing makeup?"

Jolie pointed to her chin. "Beard burn."

"Braggart." Laughing, Connie linked arms and led the way to her apartment. "You don't need to be by yourself this evening. I've got popcorn and hot chocolate waiting. I'm dying to hear *all.*"

When they were seated in the middle of Connie's fluffy faux bearskin rug, surrounded by food, Jolie said, "Okay, here goes. This story is called 'My Weekend in Paradise with a Knight in Shining Armor.'"

"Sounds like a romance to me."

"It was. It *is.*"

Jolie told her friend everything, except the good parts.

Lance had never expected to leave his heart behind in Memphis, but that's exactly what he'd done. It was one thing to tell Jolie he loved her, and quite another to feel as if the other half of him was missing. And yet two weeks of absence had hammered that lesson home.

Why should that surprise him? One look at her and all his plans for sightseeing and getting to know the real Jolie had gone up in smoke. Why did he think he could go back to Richmond and lay out plans for a long, leisurely courtship—say six months or a year?

Besides, the case he was on suddenly escalated from fact-finding to full-blown emergency. He barely had time to keep his promise to call Jolie every night, let alone plan a courtship starting with another weekend in Memphis. At the rate things were going, he'd be lucky if he saw her again in the next six months.

Still, he did call every night as promised.

The dial on his watch showed midnight when he finally got a break. "I'm getting a cup of coffee," he told his partner, then shut himself into the break room and called Jolie.

She answered on the first ring, breathless.

"Oh, hello, darling," she said. "I've been waiting for your call."

"Sorry to be so late…again. I hope I didn't wake you."

"No, I'm just sitting here listening to B. B. King's blues and studying for a Spanish test. Don't ever hesitate to call me, anytime day or night. There's nothing I love better than waking to the sound of your voice."

"How are you?"

"Great. I've finally tamed Godzilla, and I think the SPCA really likes my work. I got to help put together a TV ad campaign."

Her sweetness and unfailing good cheer settled

over him like a hug, and he longed for her with every fiber of his being.

"I knew you could do it," he said. "I'm proud of you."

"Oh, and guess what? I'm getting to work at the dog show in Phoenix on Valentine's weekend."

"Your new job?"

"No, my old. I'll be grooming."

There was a knock on the door and Lance's partner pushed it open. "Sorry to interrupt, pal, but we need you out here."

Lance nodded, and when the door closed again, said, "I'm sorry, baby, I've gotta go."

"Oh." Her disappointment sliced him straight through the heart. "Be careful, darling. I love you."

When Lance hung up he felt as if he'd cut off his life support system. As he joined his partner and the rest of the ISF team in the room filled with glowing computer screens, ringing telephones, charts, maps and cigarette smoke, he knew that he couldn't continue to maintain a telephone-only relationship. For that matter, he realized that an occasional weekend wouldn't be enough, either.

Jolie Kat Coltrane deserved more.

And so did he.

He went to his desk and checked his crowded calendar. Somehow, somewhere, there had to be time for love.

Chapter Twenty-One

Phoenix was much warmer than Memphis, and Jolie welcomed the change. She also welcomed the opportunity to work with show dogs again. Though she loved her new job with the SPCA, she realized that she didn't want to quit grooming pets altogether because that was her chance to be around animals who were not only healthy and happy, but pampered. Seeing them balanced the scale and gave her some relief from dealing with and thinking about sick, abandoned and abused animals.

In keeping with Valentine's Day, hearts and flowers decorated the coliseum where the dog show was held. If she let herself she could feel blue being alone on the most romantic day of the year. Everywhere she looked she saw symbols of love, as well as lovers—pet owners holding hands, teenagers stealing kisses when they thought nobody was looking. Shoot, even the female poodle on the station next to hers was swooning over the fine specimen Jolie was working on, a standard poodle with perfect lines and an arrogant carriage, who, according to his owners, was going to be put out to stud after this show.

He came from a long line of champions, had won many championships himself and was sure to command a high stud fee.

As she clipped and combed, Jolie talked to her canine client. "Well, Romeo, I hear you're going to have some fun after all this work is over. Oh, you didn't know. I'll let you in on a little secret, pal. There's nothing in this world as wonderful as romance. See that little poodle over there—"

Suddenly a loud clatter of hooves down the cavernous facility caught her attention. Jolie looked up to see a real live knight in genuine shining armor on a white stallion. And he was headed her way.

"Oh my." With one hand on Romeo and the other clutching the scissors, she watched as the rider drew closer. He didn't stop until he was beside her station.

"Hello, Jolie."

"Lancelot!"

Lifting his visor, he dismounted, then took her

hand. "I love you and have discovered the hard way that I can't live without you. Will you marry me?"

"Will I marry you? *Will I marry you?*" It was the most romantic, most extravagant proposal she'd ever heard of. The proposal of her dreams, straight out of a fairy tale.

"Please say yes, Jolie."

"Oh my gosh. I'm going to cry. Yes. *Yes,* I'll marry you."

He picked her up and they laughed as they tried to kiss through the opening in his helmet.

"I wanted to get down on my knees, but I'm afraid these suits aren't made for kneeling."

"It was perfect. A dream come true."

This time he took off his helmet to kiss her. And the universe moved! Actually, it was his horse, but that didn't matter, because from where she stood— in Lance's arms—she knew she was in the exact center of the universe, and that it would always move when they kissed.

A small audience gathered, and a few people clapped, but the two of them never noticed. They kissed until it was time to get Romeo ready for the show. Then later that evening, in her motel room, they took up where they'd left off.

"We have so much to talk about," she declared.

"Do we have to talk now?"

"It can wait," she told him.

And it did…for a very long time.

* * *

In May, when the irises and roses were in bloom and the sun was shining, two hundred guests arrived at O'Banyon Manor for a double wedding. Seated on folding chairs on the wide expanse of lawn facing the rose garden, they watched as members of the wedding party took their places in front of a wrought-iron, Victorian arbor covered with pink roses.

The grooms—Dr. Ben Appleton and Lancelot Shane Estes—wore tuxedos. The brides wore purple.

In a show of solidarity for Lucille O'Banyon Coltrane, Jolie came smiling down the rose-perfumed pathway behind her mother in a floor-length dress of purple chiffon with a sequined bodice, a new woman everybody expected great things from.

The bridesmaids wore pink, and since two of them had insisted on outrageous hats, Connie and Elizabeth went along, because they'd seen it was no use arguing with Kitty O'Banyon and Dolly Wilder.

The guest of honor sat on the front row with the director from the nursing home, wearing her favorite red cowboy boots. Beside them sat Clyde Shane and his wife, Lydia, who had flown in from Phoenix, and at the insistence of Kitty and Dolly would be staying on a few days as guests at O'Banyon Manor. And near the back sat Michael Sullivan, who knew a thing or two about making hell freeze over.

The Reverend Josh O'Banyon performed the ceremony, and after two sets of I do's, the newlyweds kissed none-too-sedately, which pleased the guests enormously. After all, these were Coltrane women from wild O'Banyon stock, so what else could you expect?

After the ceremony, champagne flowed freely, nobody fell in the pool and the band stayed until the last guest gave up trying to dance and went home. Dr. Ben and his wife, Lucy, departed for an extended stay in Italy. And Lancelot and his wife, Jolie, set off to board the riverboat that would take them on a leisurely honeymoon cruise from Memphis to New Orleans.

Aboard the *Memphis Belle,* Lance carried Jolie over the threshold of the honeymoon suite, which featured a canopied bed with red velvet curtains and gold fringe. She felt like a queen.

"How did you know I've always wanted to do this?" she asked.

"A little bird told me."

"Was her name Elizabeth?"

"Married only one day and already you're prying into my closely held secrets."

"You haven't seen anything yet. I plan to discover all your secrets."

When he placed her among the velvet covers and bent over her—his face open, his eyes tender and rich with promise—she fell in love all over again.

"I wouldn't want to keep you waiting, Mrs. Estes."

By the time they left their room, the moon had risen over the Mississippi and laid a path of silver across the water. Jolie leaned back in her husband's arms, sighing.

"Happy?" he asked.

"Ecstatic." Glancing up, she gave him a mischievous grin. "There is one thing missing, though."

"What's that?"

"A kitchen."

"Is there no end to your demands, Mrs. Estes?"

Laughing, he kissed her and then they walked around the deck till they came to some wide doors, where music from the riverboat's band drifted through. They danced on the deck, just the two of them alone with the moon, the music and their love. When they finally went back inside, Jolie fell asleep curved against her husband's chest.

She had no sooner closed her eyes—or so it seemed—than she felt Lance's hands sliding under her, lifting her off the bed.

"What?" she murmured. "What is it?"

"Shh. A little surprise."

He carried her through the darkened riverboat, down winding stairs and into the pristine galley done in stainless steel.

"The *kitchen.*"

"And it's all ours for the next three hours."

"Oh, Lance, how did you do it?"

He didn't answer right away, but positioned her on the cool countertop, then leaned in close and slid her gown over her head. The feel of his hands against her skin transported her to a place where only the two of them could go, a lovely secret world filled with warmth and laughter and the knowledge that as long as they loved truly and completely, they would be richly blessed.

"Magic," he finally said, and she knew it was so. Now and forever.

*   *   *   *   *

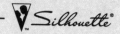

SPECIAL EDITION™

SECRET SISTERS...

Separated at birth—in mortal danger.
Three sisters find each other
and the men they were destined to love.

International bestselling author

Annette Broadrick

brings you the second of
three heartrending stories
of discovery and love.

TOO TOUGH TO TAME

Coming in December 2003

And look for MAN IN THE MIST, currently available,
and MacGOWAN MEETS HIS MATCH, coming
in January 2004, from Silhouette Special Edition

Available at your favorite retail outlet.

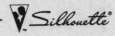

✂

Your opinion is important to us! Please take a few moments to share your thoughts with us about your experiences with Harlequin and Silhouette books. Your comments will be very useful in ensuring that we deliver books you love to read.
***Please take a few minutes to complete the questionnaire,
then send it to us at the address below.***

Send your completed questionnaires to:
Harlequin/Silhouette Reader Survey, P.O. Box 9046, Buffalo, NY 14269-9046

---

1. As you may know, there are many different lines under the Harlequin and Silhouette brands. Each of the lines is listed below. Please check the box that most represents your reading habit for each line.

Line	Currently read this line	Do not read this line	Not sure if I read this line
Harlequin American Romance	❑	❑	❑
Harlequin Duets	❑	❑	❑
Harlequin Romance	❑	❑	❑
Harlequin Historicals	❑	❑	❑
Harlequin Superromance	❑	❑	❑
Harlequin Intrigue	❑	❑	❑
Harlequin Presents	❑	❑	❑
Harlequin Temptation	❑	❑	❑
Harlequin Blaze	❑	❑	❑
Silhouette Special Edition	❑	❑	❑
Silhouette Romance	❑	❑	❑
Silhouette Intimate Moments	❑	❑	❑
Silhouette Desire	❑	❑	❑

2. Which of the following best describes why you bought *this book?* One answer only, please.

the picture on the cover	❑	the title	❑
the author	❑	the line is one I read often	❑
part of a miniseries	❑	saw an ad in another book	❑
saw an ad in a magazine/newsletter	❑	a friend told me about it	❑
I borrowed/was given this book	❑	other: _____	❑

3. Where did you buy *this book?* One answer only, please.

at Barnes & Noble	❑	at a grocery store	❑
at Waldenbooks	❑	at a drugstore	❑
at Borders	❑	on eHarlequin.com Web site	❑
at another bookstore	❑	from another Web site	❑
at Wal-Mart	❑	Harlequin/Silhouette Reader	❑
at Target	❑	Service/through the mail	
at Kmart	❑	used books from anywhere	
at another department store or mass merchandiser	❑	I borrowed/was given this book	❑

4. On average, how many Harlequin and Silhouette books do you buy at one time?

I buy _____ books at one time	❑
I rarely buy a book	❑

MRQ403SSE-1A

5. How many times per month do you shop for any *Harlequin and/or Silhouette* books?
One answer only, please.

1 or more times a week ❑	a few times per year ❑
1 to 3 times per month ❑	less often than once a year ❑
1 to 2 times every 3 months ❑	never ❑

6. When you think of your ideal heroine, which *one* statement describes her the best?
One answer only, please.

She's a woman who is strong-willed ❑	She's a desirable woman ❑
She's a woman who is needed by others ❑	She's a powerful woman ❑
She's a woman who is taken care of ❑	She's a passionate woman ❑
She's an adventurous woman ❑	She's a sensitive woman ❑

7. The following statements describe types or genres of books that you may be
interested in reading. Pick *up to 2 types* of books that you are most interested in.

I like to read about truly romantic relationships ❑
I like to read stories that are sexy romances ❑
I like to read romantic comedies ❑
I like to read a romantic mystery/suspense ❑
I like to read about romantic adventures ❑
I like to read romance stories that involve family ❑
I like to read about a romance in times or places that I have never seen ❑
Other: _____ ❑

*The following questions help us to group your answers with those readers who are
similar to you. Your answers will remain confidential.*

8. Please record your year of birth below.
19 _____

9. What is your marital status?
single ❑   married ❑   common-law ❑   widowed ❑
divorced/separated ❑

10. Do you have children 18 years of age or younger currently living at home?
yes ❑   no ❑

11. Which of the following best describes your employment status?
employed full-time or part-time ❑   homemaker ❑   student ❑
retired ❑   unemployed ❑

12. Do you have access to the Internet from either home or work?
yes ❑   no ❑

13. Have you ever visited eHarlequin.com?
yes ❑   no ❑

14. What state do you live in?
_____

15. Are you a member of Harlequin/Silhouette Reader Service?
yes ❑   Account # _____   no ❑   MRQ403SSE-1B

If you enjoyed what you just read,
then we've got an offer you can't resist!

Take 2 bestselling
love stories FREE!
Plus get a FREE surprise gift!

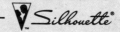

SPECIAL EDITION™

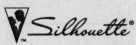

COMING NEXT MONTH.

SPECIAL EDITION

#1579 THE MARRYING MacALLISTER—
Joan Elliott Pickart
The Baby's Bet: MacAllister's Gifts
Matt MacAllister had some unusual souvenirs from his vacation to
China: a wife and twins! Caitlin Cunningham needed a temporary
husband to bring her adopted children to California. Career-minded
Matt agreed…never expecting to actually *fall* for his newfound
family! But could he truly be daddy material?

#1580 SWEET TALK—Jackie Merritt
Montana Mavericks: The Kingsleys
The spitfire with the aqua-blue eyes had been on Fire Chief
Reed Kingsley's mind for months. But Valerie Fairchild kept a
barrier of hurt between herself and the world. She didn't want
a relationship—but she couldn't ignore the flames Reed set off
whenever he was near!

#1581 TOO TOUGH TO TAME—Annette Broadrick
Secret Sisters
Drawn together through past misunderstandings, business tycoon
Dominic "Nick" Chakaris and artist Kelly MacLeod could not fight
their fierce attraction to each other. For Kelly, giving in to desire
would be a betrayal to her family. But Nick was not the type who
took "no" for an answer.…

#1582 HIS DEFENDER—Stella Bagwell
Men of the West
A murder mystery was hanging over the T Bar K, and
Ross Ketchum found himself accused of a crime he didn't
commit. His lawyer, Isabella Corrales, saw behind the wealthy
rancher's arrogance to the family man within. But she'd been
hired to defend Ross—not fall in love with him!

#1583 MAKE-BELIEVE MISTLETOE—Gina Wilkins
Men of the West
An ice storm left Professor Lucy Guerin stranded in rural
northern Arkansas with only the home of Richard Banner as shelter.
Although Banner didn't like the idea of opening his home—or his
heart—to anyone, the elfin beauty was soon
teaching the reclusive carpenter how to build trust…and love.

#1584 DADDY PATROL—Sharon De Vita
Kid-loving sheriff and local baseball coach Joe Marino received
a letter from fatherless twin boys wanting to learn how to play
baseball. Single mom Mattie Maguire cautioned her five-year-olds
about getting too attached to Joe…but could she convince her heart
to follow the same advice?